She would be less than human if she didn't resent the man who had shown her a glimpse of heaven when he touched her,

then hell when she discovered he had lied.

Damn it, Michele thought, perhaps Cord had been lying to her all along. About everything. Including the attraction he'd implied he felt for her.

Briefly, Cord had made her feel confident of her own femininity, of her desirability. And she'd reveled in the unaccustomed feeling. Her response to him had been overpowering. Explosive.

But with devastating sadness, she now realized that whatever might have been...no longer mattered.

And that bitter thought nearly brought Michele to her knees.

Dear Reader,

Welcome to Silhouette **Special Edition**...welcome to romance. Spring is here, and thoughts turn to love...so put a spring in your step for these wonderful stories this month.

We start off with our THAT SPECIAL WOMAN! title for April, *Where Dreams Have Been...* by Penny Richards. In this story, the whereabouts of a woman's lost son are somehow connected to an enigmatic man. Now she's about to find out how his dreams can help them find her missing son—and heal his own troubled past.

Also this month is *A Self-Made Man* by Carole Halston, a tale of past unrequited love that's about to change. Making the journey from the wrong side of the tracks to self-made man, this hero is determined to sweep the only woman he's ever truly loved off her feet.

To the West next for Pamela Toth's *Rocky Mountain Rancher*. He's a mysterious loner with a past...and he wants his ranch back from the plucky woman who's now running it. But complicating matters are his growing feelings of love for this tough but tender woman who has won his heart. And no visit to the West would be complete without a stop in Big Sky country, in Marianne Shock's *What Price Glory*. Paige Meredith has lived with ambition and without love for too long. Now rugged rancher Ross Tanner is about to change all that.

Don't miss Patt Bucheister's *Instant Family,* a moving story of finding love—and long-lost family—when one least expects it. Finally, debuting this month is new author Amy Frazier, with a story about a woman's return to the home she left, hoping to find the lost child she desperately seeks. And waiting there is the man who has loved her from afar all these years—and who knows the truth behind *The Secret Baby*. Don't miss it!

I hope you enjoy these books, and all the stories to come!

Sincerely,

Tara Gavin

Senior Editor

Please address questions and book requests to:
Silhouette Reader Service
U.S.: 3010 Walden Ave., P.O. Box 1325, Buffalo, NY 14269
Canadian: P.O. Box 609, Fort Erie, Ont. L2A 5X3

PATT BUCHEISTER
INSTANT FAMILY

Silhouette®

SPECIAL EDITION®

Published by Silhouette Books
America's Publisher of Contemporary Romance

I would like to thank Dr. Linda Hayles, D.V.M., and her
helpful staff—Denise, Christie, Sally and Terry—for
their generous assistance. Any technical or medical
errors are mine and in no way reflect on their expertise.

I also wish to acknowledge other adult children of
alcoholics. Today is a fresh start.

 SILHOUETTE BOOKS

ISBN 0-373-09953-3

INSTANT FAMILY

Copyright © 1995 by Patt Bucheister

Printed in U.S.A.

Books by Patt Bucheister

Silhouette Special Edition

Tilt at Windmills #773
Unpredictable #899
Instant Family #953

PATT BUCHEISTER

was born and raised in Iowa and has since lived in California, Hawaii and England. After moving nineteen times in the twenty-four years of her husband's career in the U.S. navy, she has settled permanently with her husband in Virginia Beach—near the Atlantic Ocean and her two married sons. Due to extensive traveling over the years, she has a wide range of places and locations to use in her novels.

Along with her writing, she has a variety of interests, primarily painting in her studio and learning a form of martial arts called t'ai chi ch'uan.

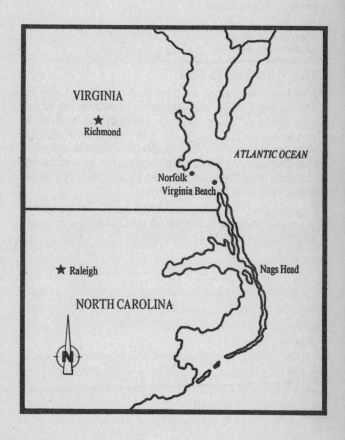

Chapter One

The warning came too late. Cord was halfway through the doorway leading to the veterinarian's waiting room when he heard a woman's voice shout at him to close the door quickly. The word *please* was tacked on at the end in a tone of voice that implied it was an order and not a polite request. Cord had no idea why it was so important to shut the door with such urgency, but he decided to act now and ask questions later.

As he started to step aside so the door could close, he saw a small bundle of brown-and-black fur bounce down a hallway toward him. Rather than accidentally step on the creature, which seemed to have the sense of direction of a Ping-Pong ball, Cord stood still.

Which meant the door didn't get closed.

Cord heard a different female voice yell, "Get him!" which made him wonder if the command was

directed toward the dog or at him for not closing the
door. As he watched the miniature dog dart in one direction, then another, like a berserk mop, Cord could
have sworn he heard the screech of a bird, a very loud
bird straight out of a National Geographic documen-
tary on the rain forest. Even more bizarre was that
Cord thought the squawking bird had said something
that sounded like "Bad boy." Since there was also
barking, meowing and a general murmuring of advice from people in the waiting room, Cord figured he
must have been mistaken.

A tiny bell attached to the dog's collar tinkled cra-
zily as the diminutive Yorkshire terrier headed toward
freedom and the great outdoors. Instead of attempt-
ing to go around the man-made barrier, the dog aimed
for the only available space directly in front of him.

Which happened to be between Cord's legs.

When Cord bent over to grab the animal, he heard
the slap of leather soles moving swiftly on the linoleum floor. The hurried footsteps were close, but he
didn't dare take his eyes off the dog to see who or what
else was hurtling in his direction. The next few seconds were a blur of colors, sounds and textures as he
attempted to grab the runaway fur ball.

Cord heard the squawking voice announce, "Bad
boy" again just as his fingers pressed against something firm and gently curved and not at all furry.

His hands adapted automatically to the lush curves
of a nicely shaped feminine rear end. He had no idea
how that happened, but there was no getting around
the fact that he was grasping a woman's nether
regions. He quickly removed his hands before she decided to forget the dog and slap his face.

But he didn't look away. It wasn't every day he literally had a woman at his feet. If she looked as interesting in the front as she did in back, this trip to Nags Head, North Carolina, wasn't going to be half the chore he had originally thought it would be. He didn't plan on missing a moment of the experience.

As he watched in bemused fascination, the woman stretched her arms out to catch the dog.

"Gotcha, Willoughby," she said in a triumphant voice as she clasped the squirming little body around his middle and started wiggling back through Cord's spread legs.

The sight of the woman's hips writhing on the floor between his legs gave Cord a few bad moments. He fought an almost irresistible desire to join her.

A few minutes earlier, he would have said that nothing could take his mind off the object of his visit to Nags Head. But he found his mind wandering into an intriguing area that had nothing to do with his mission to find his partner's estranged daughter.

A couple of leashed dogs in the waiting room added their barked opinion to the impatient yips coming from the Yorkshire terrier as their owners applauded the rescue. Laughter blended in with congratulations directed toward the woman clutching the dog.

Cord didn't move away when she sat on her heels in front of him and, with her free arm, made a sweeping motion in a mock bow.

Grinning down at the dog, she said, "Maybe we should take this act on the road, Willoughby. We're a hit."

Cord didn't notice anything or anyone except her. Willoughby could have nibbled on his ankle, and Cord wouldn't have noticed. Puzzled by his reaction, he examined her features carefully, hoping to find the reason for the odd sensation of bemused attraction he was experiencing.

The woman's expressive green eyes were glowing with amusement, their color a rich, deep jade he noticed when she glanced up at him with a smile that invited him to join in. Her expression showed no sign of embarrassment or anger—only humor, he noted.

Cord liked her reaction, although it was unexpected. None of the women he knew would have dived across the floor to rescue a dinky dog. A crisp hundred-dollar bill might have created a stir. But an undignified sprawl on the floor to catch a runaway dog wouldn't be considered a remote possibility for any woman he'd ever known.

This particular female, however, thought the situation was hilarious. He had to admit he'd thoroughly enjoyed parts of the last few moments, too.

His gaze lowered to the tiny dog nuzzling the front of her shirt. The dog's movements were pulling the pale blue material across her small, perfectly rounded breasts. The animal was making soft whimpering sounds caused by either frustration or contentment. It was difficult for Cord to tell the difference.

He was experiencing a strange blend of both himself.

Cord found himself actually feeling jealous of the dog for having the privilege of snuggling against the woman. That admission made him wonder why he was so enthralled by her. He supposed she could be called attractive, but she wasn't breathtakingly beautiful. Her figure was okay, but traffic wouldn't come to a screeching halt when she crossed a street. She was lean, trim and athletic, but certainly not voluptuously stirring to a man's blood. Yet she held his attention as no other woman had in a long time. If ever, he mused, puzzled by the strength of his reaction. He couldn't figure out why she affected him so strongly. She wasn't even close to the type of woman he usually noticed. She was certainly the opposite of his ex-wife.

That could be the main attraction, he reflected ruefully.

Cord's gaze swept over her as he looked closer for clues to explain his unsettling fascination with her. Her straight, shoulder-length blond hair was tucked casually behind her ears as though for convenience rather than as an attempt at any elaborate style. The material of her sky blue cotton shirt was wrinkled in front, thanks to the persistent burrowing of the hyperactive Yorkshire terrier. The long sleeves had been rolled up several turns to just below her elbows, exposing slender forearms and delicately boned wrists. She wore only a slim silver watch, no clanking bracelets or any rings, her fingernails unpolished and trimmed short. Her face was clean, skin porcelain smooth and completely void of makeup except for perhaps a touch of brown mascara to darken her long lashes.

Cord concluded that she reminded him of the freshly scrubbed girl-next-door most mothers would choose for their beloved sons.

Even though most teenage boys and a few older ones would undoubtedly prefer someone with a bit more spice and not quite so nice, thought Cord with a degree of cynicism and a great deal of long-term memory. He knew a number of men who shied away from the homey, pipe-and-slippers variety. He was one of them.

Not that he had a great deal of experience with that type of women, he admitted. His own mother had abandoned him at age twelve and his ex-wife had walked out after two years, preferring the latest fashions and constant partying over anything remotely domestic like cooking, cleaning or sleeping with her husband. She hadn't minded hopping into bed with other women's husbands, however.

The one time he'd ignored his vow to remain uninvolved in someone else's life had backfired so loudly when he'd married Rosemary, he wasn't about to do it again.

The sound of the woman's laughter trickled down his spine like warm rain. It didn't matter that Cord hadn't been able to think of a single reason why he was attracted to her. He just was.

And he didn't like it.

Cord closed the clinic door firmly in case any other renegade critter decided to make a run for it. Then he extended his hand toward her. She looked at it as though she'd never seen one before.

When she brought her puzzled gaze back to meet his, he asked casually, "Am I breaking some kind of feminist rule by offering to help you up?"

She shook her head, smiled and clasped his fingers. "If you are, I'm not aware of which rule it would be. I thought you wanted to take the dog." A few seconds later, she was standing in front of him. She needed both hands to control the wiggling little dog and quickly released his hand. "Thanks for your help."

He shrugged. "I didn't do anything. If it wasn't for you, the dog would be long gone by now."

"I meant for helping me to my feet."

"Anytime," he murmured absently, his concentration wavering when he noticed flecks of gold shining in her amused green eyes.

She looked away when a younger woman wearing a royal blue baseball jacket came down a hallway toward them. A white oval patch on the left front of the jacket had Sand Dune Animal Hospital embroidered on it with glossy black thread. On the other side, the name Dixie was sewn in white script letters.

Her attention was on the woman holding the dog. "Do you want me to take Willoughby back to the examination room for you?"

Shaking her head, the woman said, "I'll bring him in. Thanks anyway." She turned back to Cord. "I hope you aren't put off by the chaos. It's usually not like this around here."

Dixie grinned. "Sometimes it's worse."

With an amused quirk of her mouth, the lady with the dog admitted, "It does get a little hectic sometimes. But all evidence to the contrary, your pet will get good care here."

Realizing she must think he was a potential customer, Cord nodded briefly in acknowledgment rather than explain his real reason for coming to the clinic.

She turned and walked away beside Dixie, disappearing into one of the doorways off the hallway, which he guessed was an examination room. Since she wasn't wearing a nylon jacket, which apparently was a uniform of sorts for the clinic staff, the intriguing woman who'd spent too short a time between his legs must be the dog's owner, he guessed.

A few people smiled in his direction when he stepped over to the check-in counter built into a wall facing the door. On either side of the counter were glass-fronted display units with an assortment of shampoo, flea and tick sprays, and other pet-related ointments and salves on shelves that ran from floor to ceiling.

An older woman wearing the uniform jacket and a plastic name tag in the shape of a cat that announced her name was Gail looked up and smiled. "Can I help you?"

"I'd like to see Michele LaBrock."

She frowned as she scanned the typed list of appointments. "Do you have an appointment?"

He shook his head. "No. I don't."

She looked up. "Is this an emergency?"

Cord realized that from her position behind the counter, she couldn't see below his waist to the floor. She obviously assumed he had brought in an animal to be treated.

"It's not an emergency the way you mean, but it's important that I talk to Miss LaBrock as soon as possible."

Emphasizing the veterinarian's title, she said, "*Dr.* LaBrock has had a full schedule of appointments all afternoon." The woman glanced down again at the appointment book spread out in front of her. After a few seconds had ticked by, she raised her gaze to his. "You're in luck today, though. There haven't been any emergencies, so she should be finished with her regular appointments by five if you care to wait."

Cord glanced at his watch, which told him he would have to waste at least twenty minutes. "I'll hang around as long as it takes."

If Gail heard the determined edge in his voice, she didn't let on. "If you'll give me your name, I'll put you down for the last appointment."

"Cord Thomas."

He could visualize the woman running his name through her mental filing system. She squinted, frowned and bit her bottom lip while her inner data bank churned away.

He helped her out. "I left a message last week for her to call me. She never did."

A puzzled frown creased the woman's brow. "If you had left a message for Dr. LaBrock to return your call, she would have done exactly that. She's extremely conscientious and efficient."

"The purpose of the call had nothing to do with her profession."

The receptionist blinked twice, surprise widening her eyes. "I'm sure I would have remembered a personal call from a man for Dr. LaBrock. There aren't that many."

Cord smiled faintly at the horrified look on the receptionist's face when she realized what she had revealed about her employer. He watched the woman to see what reaction he would get from her when he asked his next question.

"The message was for Michele Sutherland, not Michele LaBrock."

Gail gave him a look that could have withered fresh lettuce. "Well, no wonder she didn't return your call, Mr. Thomas. You asked for the wrong person."

He didn't tell her that he wished she was right. If that was the case, he wouldn't have had to drive for two hours from Virginia Beach, Virginia, to Nags Head. Doing his own work plus his partner's left him with very little free time. As it was, he hadn't been able to leave as early as he'd planned. The truck bringing frozen bait from Florida to the marina had had a faulty refrigeration unit and all the packages of Ballyhoo were spoiled. Arranging for substitute bait to supply the charter boats had taken time.

Gail had inadvertently confirmed the findings of his partner's private investigator. Michele Sutherland didn't use her real last name.

Cord didn't like being in the middle of his partner's family feud or whatever the hell it was that was going on between Michael and his daughter. The ingredients that went into making a family were as mysterious to Cord as the unexplained disappearances of ships in the Bermuda Triangle. And he didn't want anything to do with that problem, either.

But he did believe in being loyal to a friend.

"I have the correct person," he said more brusquely than he'd intended. His tone did not encourage questions. "I'd like to talk to Miss LaBrock as soon as she's free."

Gail penciled in his name at the bottom of the page. Emphasizing the veterinarian's title again, she said, "*Dr.* LaBrock will see you when she can."

He nodded and turned away. Glancing around, he looked for a place to sit down. A brown tweed-patterned carpet covered benches that had been built along the front of the waiting room on either side of the entrance. They extended along ten feet of the connecting walls for people and animals to use. Cord guessed the examination rooms were situated off the two hallways located on either side of the built-in glass cases and the check-in counter.

Cord chose a space next to a husky bearded man dressed in black leather; he was holding a tiny Chihuahua in the palm of his huge callused hand, with the leash wrapped around fingers the size of sausages. A petite elderly woman gripping the leash connected to a huge Great Dane sitting at her feet was seated on the man's right.

Cord sat and leaned against the wall. He wasn't in the mood for small talk and purposely stared at the glass cases in front of him rather than at the other people waiting to see the vet. An elderly woman was seated on the bench that extended at a right angle along the wall several feet away. She had been chatting with the owner of the Great Dane and was evidently curious why Cord was there without an animal.

She had come to her own conclusion and had decided to share it with him whether he wanted her to or not. "If you're here to check out Dr. LaBrock before you bring your pet in, Mrs. Turner and I will gladly give you references if that would help. Won't we, Gladys?"

Both the huge dog and his little owner glanced at Cord. "I wouldn't take Frisco to see anyone else except Dr. LaBrock," she said in a soft voice Cord had to strain to hear. "She's a very caring person. Frisco doesn't like to be fussed with, but Dr. LaBrock has him eating out of her hand."

Cord glanced at the Great Dane. He could easily visualize the dog taking off the vet's hand with one bite. His gaze returned to the other woman. A mutt of indiscriminate breeding was sitting near her feet. Not feet, but a single foot, he realized. The left leg of her brown slacks was folded and pinned back just below the knee. A pair of crutches were leaning against the bench on her left. Something about the dog caught Cord's attention next, and he saw that the animal was also missing a leg. The front left leg. He found the similarity between pet and owner to be oddly poignant.

Hoping to find out something more about his partner's daughter that hadn't been included in the investigator's report, he started with, "How long has Dr. LaBrock had her practice in Nags Head?"

The woman with the three-legged dog furnished the answer. "Let's see . . . It must be four years now. She started out in a small clinic in a shopping mall until her practice grew to the point that she required more room. Gladys and I have brought our dogs to her almost from the beginning."

"From the beginning," murmured Gladys with a decisive nod of her head.

"To give you an idea of how kind the dear girl is," the other woman continued, "she came to my house shortly after my surgery in order to check on Teenie when she had her puppies. I couldn't take them in to the clinic to be checked, you see, so Dr. LaBrock made a house call. She's such a sweet girl."

"Very sweet," echoed Gladys.

"She stayed for over an hour just to keep me company. She came back when it was time for their shots later and brought an African violet to add to my collection. Wasn't that nice of her?"

"Very nice," contributed Gladys.

Cord was beginning to feel like a spectator at a tennis match as he looked back and forth between the two women as they batted the conversation around.

Teenie's owner served the next ball. "She's been in this location for over two years now. She's so busy, she's taken on a partner to help with the work load. Bud Jameson is a nice boy, but Teenie and I prefer Dr. LaBrock."

Cord let his gaze roam vaguely over the glass cases and the tidy waiting room. The beige linoleum floor gleamed brightly under the fluorescent overhead lighting.

"The clinic seems to be well equipped."

"Oh, it is. There are kennels in the back, a modern surgery and eight examination rooms," supplied his willing informant. She then added for good measure, "The people who work here are all highly trained technicians who clearly love animals."

A plump calico cat came ambling down one of the halls toward them. He hopped up on the bench, gave Cord a bored look with half-closed eyes, then curled into a ball for a nap.

The elderly woman chuckled. "That's Boots. He lives here."

Cord stared at the cat. "He lives in the clinic?"

She nodded, grinning broadly at his surprised expression. "So does a kitten and a gray cat. They all have the run of the place." She glanced toward the opposite end of the room. "Shylock lives here, too."

Cord followed the direction of her gaze and noticed a large cage hanging from the ceiling in the corner. He didn't know how he could have missed it. The wire-and-bamboo cage would have barely fit into the galley of his boat, it was so big. A black macaw with a bright yellow beak stared back at Cord through the strands of wire.

As though aware he was the center of attention, the bird squawked loudly, "Bad boy."

"He really is sometimes," Gladys said with a smile. "Shylock knows a few swearwords he picked up from his previous owner. He learned to say 'bad boy' because that's what Dr. LaBrock calls him when he swears." Getting back to the original topic of conversation, at least on her part, she asked, "Have you just recently moved to Nags Head?"

He shook his head. The reason for his presence in the vet's waiting room was too complicated to go into even if he wanted to, which he didn't. It might have been interesting to see how the curious women would take the explanation that he was there to persuade Dr. LaBrock to see her father for the first time in twenty-six years.

The two women gave him curious looks, but before either one could launch any further inquisitions, the technician named Dixie returned to the waiting room.

"Okay, Frisco," she said to the Great Dane. "Let's get you weighed."

It was a toss-up whether the dog led petite Gladys down the hallway or the other way around, Cord observed with amusement.

A minute later, the woman and her three-legged dog were called in by a staff member Cord hadn't seen before. She was wearing a blue jacket like the others but was too far away for Cord to be able to read her embroidered name. The number of personnel he'd seen so far confirmed the older woman's opinion that Dr. LaBrock had a substantial practice.

The technician patiently waited while the dog's owner wrapped the leash around her wrist and arranged her crutches into position. When the woman stood, the dog did, too, as if by some silent signal. With an odd dignity that made Cord smile, the mutt hobbled ahead of his owner, on three legs, toward the technician.

Inside examination room 4, the Yorkshire terrier remained under duress on the high stainless-steel table, his brief bid for freedom a thing of the past. His owner, Bruce Denham, stood on one side facing Michele, who was finally able to finish the postoperative examination on Willoughby.

The dog's owner needed more reassurance than the animal did, so Michele made a point to give it. "As I told you earlier, Mr. Denham, Willoughby has fully recovered from the surgery without any complications. The safety pin he swallowed caused a blockage, but luckily the pin was closed and not open." Her gentle fingers passed over the small incision scar left from the stitches she'd removed prior to Willoughby's escape a few moments ago. "His leap off the table and his race toward the door should prove to you that he's back to his old perky self."

The tension visibly eased between the man's shoulders, and he ran his hand over his pet's back. "He did tear out of here with his usual energy, didn't he?"

She nodded, her eyes amused as she looked down at the cause of the commotion, who gazed back at her with big innocent black eyes. "If the man in the doorway hadn't slowed him down by being in his way, Willoughby would still be running, and we would still be chasing."

Bruce glanced down at the white Fiberglas walking cast running from below his knee to his toes, which was visible between the split seam in his slacks. "I wasn't much help, was I?"

Michele gave Willoughby a doggie treat. "No harm was done to either your dog or the man in the doorway, so don't worry about it."

She might as well have told him to stop breathing. Fretting was something she knew the middle-aged man excelled in. Even when everything was going smoothly, the accountant would be concerned that there was nothing to worry about.

"Are you sure the man who helped save Willoughby wasn't hurt? Some people sue for the slightest of reasons."

The image of the man in the doorway was astonishingly clear in Michele's mind. Usually nothing came between her and her work, but he had hovered in the background of her thoughts ever since she'd taken his outstretched hand.

"I'm positive you won't have to call your lawyer. The guy seemed to take the whole incident in stride." She glanced at the technician who was entering the examination room with Willoughby's medication in her hand. "Dixie, you saw the man who Willoughby chose to use as a tunnel near the front door. Assure Mr. Denham that the guy hasn't been harmed in any way."

Setting the vial of medication next to Willoughby's chart on the cabinet, the young woman smiled at the dog's owner. "If the man was in any better shape, I'd propose." To Michele, she added, "I might as well confess. We're taking turns with the appointments so everyone can have a good look at him."

The open candor of her young staff was always a source of fascination to Michele, who had never experienced their confident lighthearted approach to life. But on the other hand, they hadn't been exposed to the joy and delight of taking care of someone else at a time in their lives when someone should have been taking care of them. Michele dismissed the maudlin self-pity she rarely indulged in. She hooked Willoughby's leash to his collar. "I hope no one is being too obvious. The man must already have an odd opinion of how we operate after I dove between his legs to catch Willough-by. Being gawked at by the staff might not sit too well with him.''

"He doesn't even notice us," the technician said with more than a little disgust. "He sees us, but we don't appear to make much of an impression, if you know what I mean. Those gray eyes sort of looked right through me."

Michele didn't know what Dixie meant. Her impression had been that the man had tried to see into her soul with the intensity of a laser beam. His effect on her puzzled her. Physically, he was moderately attractive, his black hair and gray eyes a stunning combination. But it was more than appearance, she decided. He had a presence that was oddly compelling in an undefinable way, which bothered her all the more when she couldn't find a plausible reason for her reaction. Michele preferred clear concise explanations and evidence to support the conclusions she reached. Neither were available in this particular case.

She gently stroked the Yorkshire terrier's head and gave his owner instructions to go along with the medication. She accepted Mr. Denham's profuse thanks with a smile that hid her irritation about being unable to get the man in the waiting room off her mind.

He had probably forgotten about her the minute she was out of sight, she chided herself.

Cord heard the tinkling bell first. He frowned in irritation when his body tensed with anticipation of seeing Willoughby's owner again. The little Yorkshire terrier came down the far hallway, straining against the constraints of a leash attached to his collar. Cord raised his eyes to the hand that came into view and was disappointed to see masculine fingers gripping the leash.

The man hobbling awkwardly behind Willoughby appeared to be searching for something or someone as his gaze darted around the waiting room. Cord soon found out he was the man's target when Willoughby and his owner headed in his direction.

He stood when the other man switched the leash to his left hand and extended his right toward Cord. "I want to thank you for your part in preventing Willoughby from escaping. I'm Bruce Denham—his owner. He has recently had surgery and could have been in some difficulty if he'd been able to run free."

Cord accepted the man's handshake and his gratitude. "How did you know it was me?"

"Dr. LaBrock described you and mentioned that Willoughby would have gotten away if you hadn't blocked the exit."

Cord would have given a day's marina receipts to have heard what the green-eyed woman had told the vet. Then it occurred to him what the other man had said. The meaning behind the statement changed a few perceptions.

"The woman who caught your dog was Dr. La-Brock?"

Giving Cord a puzzled look, Bruce Denham nodded. "She evidently didn't take the time to introduce herself."

"Evidently."

"I do appreciate your effort."

"Glad to have helped, although I didn't do much except stand in the way."

"Thanks just the same."

Willoughby darted back and forth from Cord's deck shoes to the wall to Mr. Denham's cast-encased foot, until his owner pulled on the leash to draw the dog toward the door.

Cord watched the kinetic creature and his owner leave the waiting room, smiling faintly when Willoughby nearly tripped up the man who bought his doggie biscuits, by dashing around his foot, effectively tangling up the leash.

When the owner and his dog finally made it to their car safely and drove away, Cord sat down to think about the woman he'd been trying not to think about. Fate had suddenly made a simple request more complicated by placing an intriguing woman smack-dab in his way. This woman had captivated him since diving between his legs. She was the woman he'd come to see.

She was Michele LaBrock.

Chapter Two

Cord was relieved that the man with the Chihuahua didn't seem inclined to make conversation. Cord had more than a few things on his mind, plus more bits of information to digest than he'd had before he arrived at the Sand Dune Animal Hospital.

Had it only been fifteen minutes ago? he asked himself, finding it hard to believe.

During the drive from Virginia to the Outer Banks of North Carolina, he'd debated about the right approach he should take to persuade Michele LaBrock to see her father. The facts he had didn't make his task any easier.

She obviously had made a successful life for herself without requiring Michael's financial support. Or any other assistance, apparently. He could tell Michael she'd gotten along just fine. Then maybe his partner would get over this guilt trip he'd suddenly decided to take.

According to the investigator's report, Michele's mother was dependent on her daughter and apparently had been for a number of years, although at one time Faith LaBrock Sutherland had been an elementary school teacher who had worked her way up to assistant vice principal. Since Michael's ex-wife wasn't the person being investigated, Cord didn't know why the woman no longer held a teaching position and relied on her daughter to provide her room and board, car and all living expenses. According to the investigator, the two women didn't live together which Cord had thought was odd. They lived in separate cottages more than walking distance apart. Michael's ex-wife hadn't remarried, nor was she currently involved with any man according to the report. She depended solely on her daughter.

Cord tamped down his curiosity concerning the exchange in roles. So the child had become the parent. The reason for the switch was none of his business.

There were other factors to think about that were real and not guesswork. Michele didn't use her father's name, nor, according to Michael, had she seen him or made any attempt to contact him since she was a small child, but then, to be fair, his partner hadn't made much of an effort in the past from what Cord had gathered from the few things Michael had let slip.

Cord had no reason to believe Michele Sutherland would jump at the chance to drop everything and visit her father after all this time just because Michael asked for her. Nor could Cord think of a convincing reason to give her other than a sick man wanted to see his daughter soon in case he didn't get another chance.

Somehow Cord had to keep his personal feelings out of the negotiations with Michael's daughter. Because of his own background, he had a strong dislike for people who could turn their backs on family. Maybe Michele LaBrock had her reasons for shutting her father out of her life, but Cord's history made it difficult for him to sympathize with her. If she hadn't ignored Michael's recent attempts to reconcile their relationship by returning his letters, Cord would have been more willing to meet her with an open mind. When he'd left messages on her answering machine and at the clinic for her to return his call, he hadn't received even one phone call from her.

His loyalty was with his partner, and that was the only reason he had agreed to talk to Michael's daughter in the first place.

Cord knew why he was sitting in a vet's waiting room but not how to approach Michael's long-lost daughter.

He hadn't come up with anything brilliant to say by the time Frisco trotted out with Mrs. Turner in tow. The older lady gave him a shy smile of appreciation when he got up to open the door for her. The dog sniffed loudly, which could have meant anything from "nice to see you again" to "good riddance," and left with his owner without taking a bite out of any of Cord's vital parts.

Shortly afterward, the black-leather-attired man and his tiny dog were called back to one of the examination rooms.

Finally it was Cord's turn. The technician with the name Karen embroidered on her jacket didn't insist on the weigh-in, which was the usual procedure for patients. Instead of being shown into one of the examination rooms, he was ushered into what was obviously Dr. LaBrock's office. Cord took three steps into the room. If he'd taken two more, he would have run into the bookcase that was against the opposite wall. He glanced around, surprised by the lack of space. He had more room when he took a shower on his boat. Well, he thought, that might be a slight exaggeration, but not by much.

A wooden chair with armrests was positioned in front of a cluttered desk, and he sat on it. The only other chair was on the other side of the desk, and a coiled bundle of fur was lying on the fabric seat cushion. A man used to living on a boat, Cord was accustomed to small places, but the Sand Dune Animal Hospital was three times the size of his forty-five-foot trawler. Michele LaBrock had a lot more room to play with, yet she hadn't allotted much space for her office. Evidently, she didn't believe in pampering herself. The animals she treated had much more room than she did and probably were more comfortable.

The cluttered condition of her desk was a clue that she didn't spend much time in the office tending to paperwork. Cord could sympathize. Taking care of never-ending stacks of business forms, contracts and other necessary—but irritating—reams of paper was his least favorite thing to do. The computer Michael had insisted on buying helped some, but the paper continued to accumulate before its information was fed to the computer.

A poster showing Noah's Ark nearly overflowing with animals was in a silver-toned metal frame hanging behind the vet's chair. Cord leaned forward to read the caption underneath. Call The Vet. Someone's Got To Clean Up The Mess In The Bottom Of This Boat.

He had another tidbit to add to his growing knowledge of Michele LaBrock. She apparently had a sense of humor. She was going to need it, he thought, although he didn't think she would find the purpose of his visit very funny.

A drawing by a child of perhaps four or five years of age was tacked to the wall depicting various types of critters, some recognizable, others of an uncertain breed. All sorts of decorations had been drawn and colored on each one. Across the top was printed Animal Krakers, then a stick figure of a person with a stethoscope hanging around its neck labeled Doc LaBrock, implying the vet was crackers about animals.

Cord wondered if the good doctor of veterinary medicine felt the same way about people.

His attention was diverted from his examination of the office by the sound of voices. Karen hadn't closed the door after showing him in, and Cord could easily hear the conversation going on in the examination room next door, primarily because the occupants were arguing.

He recognized one of the feminine voices as belonging to the woman who had spent a few interesting moments between his legs. Even though her voice was definitely not amused like before, he knew it was hers. His earlier suspicions were confirmed. The woman who had piqued his interest was the reason for his hasty trip to Nags Head. She was Michael's daughter.

He didn't feel an ounce of guilt for eavesdropping on her conversation. He had nothing to do with the doors being left open and was not responsible for the argument. He did have a good excuse for hearing what she had to say. The more he knew about her, the better prepared he would be when he met her.

He heard her say, "We don't euthanize a healthy animal just because it has stained an expensive Oriental rug, Mrs. Frost. It's not unusual for a puppy to have accidents indoors while being trained."

"That animal came with a superior pedigree and a high price tag," a different female answered in a voice frigid with indignation. "I expected the dog to behave accordingly."

"An impressive pedigree and costing a lot of money has nothing to do with an animal's behavior, Mrs. Frost." After a short pause, she added, "Or a human's."

Cord grinned.

Mrs. Frost didn't see anything funny in Dr. La-Brock's attitude. "I am quite serious about getting rid of this dog, Dr. LaBrock. It was sold to me under false pretenses. The breeder assured me it would make an outstanding pet. I have seen no signs of that happening. Only disgusting messes in my house."

"The dog will be a wonderful pet once he learns to control his natural functions, Mrs. Frost. That requires some patience and training on the owner's part."

"If I'd known how much trouble this creature would be, I would never have bought it for my husband's birthday."

The vet's heartfelt sigh could be heard by Cord in the next room. "I could ask one of my technicians to explain several techniques to help you train the puppy that would prevent any further accidents. There are several methods you could try. The German shepherd breed is very intelligent. With a little effort on your part, you will have that special pet you wanted."

"I would rather you just put the animal down, Dr. LaBrock. Give it a shot or something. I will pay whatever fee you charge. I don't have the time to spend catering to a stupid dog."

Each word Dr. LaBrock spoke was with cool control. "If you agree to leave the puppy here, Mrs. Frost, we will find a new home for him, but I refuse to euthanize an animal just because he stained a rug. I don't know of any veterinarian who would. We could help find a new home for him, though, if you really don't want him."

"And how much will that cost? I've already spent a fortune on shots and tests for this animal as it is, which you were quite happy to give him and charge me for without any qualms, I might add. That doesn't include the outrageous amount I paid for the creature to begin with."

"There will be no charge for finding the dog a new home, Mrs. Frost."

Cord smiled to himself as he heard the barely checked temper in the vet's voice. His smile faded. He'd been so absorbed in the conversation taking place in the next room, he hadn't thought about the difference it made that the voice belonged to the person he'd come to see, who was also the woman he found oddly intriguing.

The brief incident between them earlier shouldn't make a difference when he finally came face-to-face with Michael's daughter. But somehow, Cord knew it would.

His heart rate had soared ridiculously high when she'd only smiled at him. He didn't understand why, but one thing he did know was that his little jaunt to Nags Head had just become more complicated. She wasn't at all what he'd expected. Instead of a faceless, cold woman who could shut her own father out of her life with apparent ease when he tried to contact her, she was a warm, obviously caring woman with animals. He had to wait to see how compassionate she would be toward her father. The preconceived picture of her he'd created in his mind was now out of focus. Instead of looking at only Michael's point of view, he would give her the benefit of the doubt.

Growing up without a father couldn't have been easy for her. Considering his own background, Cord was the last person to blame someone else for resenting being abandoned.

Cord's earlier plan to demand she see her father might have worked with the type of woman he'd originally thought her to be after Michael had told Cord about his letters being returned unopened. Now Cord had the impression this woman couldn't be pressured into doing anything she didn't want to do. Taking a trip to Virginia Beach to see Michael Sutherland might turn out to be the last thing she felt like doing.

Cord remembered one of Rocky's many gems of wisdom was that the time to abandon ship was when it was below sea level. Until then you bailed like hell. Cord knew a great deal about staying afloat, so he would stay on the course he'd charted. Until she either went along for the ride . . .

Or bombed him out of the water.

When he heard someone enter the room just behind him, he stood up and slowly turned around. Michele's expression was polite but distant as she walked into her office. She was drying her hands with a paper towel. A stethoscope was draped casually around her neck.

"I'm sorry to keep you waiting," she said as she finished wiping her hands.

He hoped the coolness in her green eyes was due to the unpleasant dog owner she'd just dealt with and not because of him.

"No problem. I appreciate your seeing me on such short notice."

She tossed the crumpled towel into a receptacle as she passed it. Standing with the desk between them, she extended her right hand toward him. Giving him a socially acceptable smile, she said, "We didn't have a chance for introductions earlier. I'm Michele La-Brock."

Cord was hesitant about taking her hand. Every male nerve in his body was screaming a warning not to touch her in any way, even in a polite, formal handshake.

Stalling, he flicked a glance at the framed official document from the school of veterinary medicine that was hanging on the wall.

"The resident vet."

"One of them," she said easily, smiling faintly as she waited for him to take her hand.

He finally clasped her hand, surprised by the jolt of energy suddenly flowing up his arm from their connected hands. Damn, he thought. This wasn't supposed to be happening.

A few seconds went by before it occurred to him something more was expected from him than a handshake.

"Cord Thomas," he murmured.

Withdrawing her hand when he didn't immediately release it, she gestured toward the chair politely with a casual flick of her wrist. "Please sit down, Mr. Thomas." When he continued to stand and stare, she said soothingly, "If you don't, I'll feel I can't, and I'd like to get off my feet for a few minutes. I'm wearing a new pair of shoes that felt terrific when I tried them on in the store but have lost their charm after eight hours."

Cord was pleased to discover he could actually function like a reasonably normal person and sat in the chair he'd occupied a moment ago.

"From what I could hear, Mrs. Frost has a lot in common with your shoes. If she ever had any charm to begin with, she doesn't have much left over when it comes to her husband's dog. What did she finally decide to do about the puppy?"

Michele bent down to pick something off her chair, which turned out to be a kitten. Setting the sleepy cat on a pile of folders where he promptly returned to his nap, she reached for a container of hand lotion after she sat down.

As she worked the cream into her skin, her gaze moved to the opened door for a second. "The examination rooms aren't very big, so I like to leave the doors open when I can. Maybe I should change my routine around here."

"Or stop taking on clients like Mrs. Frost," he commented.

The chair creaked softly when she leaned back. With a heartfelt sigh, she kicked the expensive but uncomfortable leather loafers off so they were no longer binding her feet.

Wiggling her toes in relief, she shrugged. "Animals aren't responsible for the behavior of their owners."

"So you treat the animals in spite of their owners?"

"Most of the people who have pets love and care for them. The decision to euthanize an elderly, ill animal is extremely difficult for people who love them. Having an animal destroyed because it barks, claws the furniture or leaves hair on the sofa, however, is against my principles. Some pet owners have different opinions." She removed her stethoscope and placed it on the corner of the desk. "Is that why you're here, Mr. Thomas? To check on my tolerance level of owners?"

"Not exactly." She had given him the opening to bring up the reason he was there. He hesitated taking it, although if asked why, he wouldn't have been able to give a reason that made any sense. "You haven't said what happened to Mrs. Frost's expensive pedigreed puppy."

Michele's lips formed a mocking smile. "You wouldn't be in the market for a sweet, healthy male German shepherd, would you?"

The shape of her gently curved mouth held his attention longer than he liked. "Sorry. I live on a boat. There's barely enough room for me."

"It was worth a try," she murmured. "Since you obviously don't have a pet already and don't plan on getting one, I'm curious why you want to see me. Gail said you mentioned you were here for personal reasons and not professional. Since we've never met before today, I can't even guess what it could be that you want from me."

"Do you always automatically assume someone wants something from you?"

Resting her elbows on the arms of her chair, she pressed the tips of the fingers of each hand together to form a steeple. "Usually people who walk in here without an animal or an appointment are either selling pet products, life insurance or pharmaceuticals, or want free advice about what kind of pet they should buy. It's a fair assumption to make that you want something."

"None of the above, although you're right. I do want something."

She gave him a tolerant smile. "I thought you might. I'd appreciate it if you would get to it, Mr. Thomas. I still have a few things to do before I can go home to soak my feet."

"I'm here as a favor to my partner, Michael Sutherland." She didn't blink, turn pale or give any indication at all that the mention of Michael Sutherland was disturbing. "He's very ill and would like to see you. He's only two hours away up the coast in Virginia Beach, in case you weren't aware of that. If we leave now, I could get you back here around midnight tonight."

"Is there any particular reason why your partner wants to see me?" she asked politely.

"I thought that was obvious."

Michele barely managed to refrain from letting her breath out in an irritated sigh. After the last few minutes with Mrs. Frost, her patience was worn thin, and she still had postoperative patients to see before she could go home. She wasn't in the mood for playing games.

"It might be obvious to you but not to me. Let's approach this from another angle. What type of work do you and your partner do?"

"We own a marina and charter fishing fleet of six boats, plus a restaurant in Virginia Beach."

She wasn't any wiser.

"Does your partner live on a boat, too?"

Cord had the distinct feeling he was being humored. "Michael lives in a house. Why?"

"I was just making conversation since I don't know where this is going. I'm sorry your partner is ill, Mr. Thomas, but I don't understand what that has to do with me. I'm a doctor of veterinary medicine like the diploma says. Unless your partner is a St. Bernard, I can't treat him."

"He doesn't need your professional services," he said irritably.

"Now you've really got me confused. Why does your partner want to see me?"

"Isn't it natural for a father to want to see his daughter when there is a chance he might die?"

Her eyes widened at the hard edge in his voice. "I suppose it is. You still haven't explained why Mr.... I'm sorry. I forgot his name."

"Sutherland," he snapped. "Michael Sutherland."

"Why would Mr. Sutherland want to see me now or any other time? Am I supposed to know his daughter?"

"You know her very well," murmured Cord in a rough voice. "You *are* his daughter."

Chapter Three

Michele stared at the man in her office for a few seconds. Then she glanced at the door, relieved to see she had left it open. If she needed to yell for help, someone could hear her easily enough and come to her rescue. She brought her gaze back to the man who looked perfectly sane but appeared to have lost his mind.

It was a shame such an attractive man had to be a wacko, she thought with more than an ounce of regret.

A real pity, she reflected as she remembered the glint of amusement in his gray eyes when he'd helped her to her feet after her unorthodox lunge through his legs. She liked people with a sense of humor.

She also preferred them to be in their right minds.

She studied him more thoroughly. He had strong features and a tall, lean physique that had caught her attention earlier. His dark hair was slightly tousled as though gently teased by ocean breezes more often than disciplined with a fine-toothed comb, the length brushing the collar of his blue-and-green-plaid shirt. His square jaw gave the impression of stubbornness without any indication of the possibility of a gentle nature behind it. She wondered just how obstinate he was going to be.

There were more than adequate medical facilities in the area, but she didn't know of anyplace to call that would have a straitjacket on hand.

"You're in the wrong place, and you have the wrong person, Mr. Thomas," she said quietly. "My last name is LaBrock, not Sutherland."

"Your name is Michele Diana LaBrock Sutherland. LaBrock is your mother's maiden name. Both you and your mother have gone by LaBrock since the divorce. Your birth date is January third, twenty-eight years ago."

She frowned when he stated her correct middle name and age. "I don't know where you've been getting your information, but I'm not the person you think I am. I don't know any Michael Sutherland. I'm certainly not his daughter. My father died when I was two years old."

It was Cord's turn to look at her as though she was a few pennies short of a nickel. "I talked to Michael a couple of hours ago, before I left Virginia Beach. He's still weak from a heart attack, but he is very much alive."

"I'm sure he appreciates that," she said pleasantly. "I don't understand what his physical condition has to do with me. I'm not a medical doctor as I've already mentioned."

"I told you. He's your father, and he wants to see you."

"And I told you that you have me mixed up with someone else, Mr. Thomas." Her mouth twisted into a rueful grimace. "You'll have to take my word for it, but I would have noticed growing up with a father in the house. There wasn't one. There was only my mother and me."

Cord wondered if he was imagining the brief shadow clouding her vibrant eyes for a few seconds. "Michael hasn't seen you since you were two years old," he persisted. "I don't know why. As far as I'm concerned, it doesn't matter. He wants to see you now, and I promised to bring you to him."

"Mr. Thomas," she said with as much forbearance as she could muster. "You obviously understand English, so that can't be the problem. I'll say this again if it will help. I'll even put it in writing. I don't know this Michael Sutherland. I don't know anyone by that name. I've certainly never heard of him. I'm not his long-lost daughter. I'm sorry he is ill, but I won't pretend to be someone I'm not to make you or him feel better."

"Whether you admit it or not, you're his daughter. Michael went to a lot of trouble and expense to make sure he had found the right person. Shortly after his heart attack, when it occurred to him he might be running out of time, he hired a private investigator. He wasn't able to search for you himself due to his health problems." Cord was fascinated by the glint of anger shining in her eyes at the mention of a private investigator. She wasn't going to like the rest of what he had to say, either. "Michael gave the investigator some legal documents and every bit of information he could remember about you and your mother.''

''Like what?'' she asked suddenly.

Cord's gaze narrowed at the clipped tone of her voice. Her expression gave nothing away, yet he sensed a guarded wariness. And a touch of anger. It was in her eyes. Hot, green ice, he decided, fascinated by her reaction.

In a reasonable voice, he said, ''Information like physical characteristics—hair, eyes, that sort of thing. Your mother's occupation as a schoolteacher. Your last known address. Friends, neighbors, people who worked with your mother.''

If he wasn't watching her so intently, he might have missed the momentary flicker of her lashes as she glanced away for a split second. His mind reflected back on what he'd said to her but couldn't come up with any comment that could have caused the flash of alarm he was sure he'd seen.

His voice lost some of the aggression present a moment ago. ''I didn't read the whole report, but Michael told me the investigator provided him with your present home address, where you work, what you do to support yourself and your mother, and that you and your mother use her maiden name rather than Sutherland.''

''I don't like being spied on,'' she said tightly.

''I don't blame you. I wouldn't like it, either, but in this case, it was necessary. Neither you nor your mother have taken the trouble to stay in touch with Michael over the years. What else could he do?''

It was Michele's turn to raise a brow at the hint of condemnation in his tone. ''He could have hired a competent detective while he was at it. The one he chose has taken a wrong turn somewhere along the way. Nothing you've said has proved this Michael Sutherland is my father."

"Your first name is a feminine version of Michael's name."

Michele looked down at her hands in case she didn't manage to hide the shock jolting through her like an earthquake. Her mother had said she was named after her father, Michael LaBrock.

She raised her head. "If that's supposed to prove this man is my father, it needs work."

Cord gave her a quelling glance and continued, "Once Michael had your address, he wrote to you explaining who he was and that he would like to see you when he got out of the hospital. He sent another letter when he was finally released from the hospital. You didn't answer that one either. They were returned unopened, which Michael took as a slap in the face."

"If your friend addressed the letters to Michele Sutherland, it's not surprising I never got them. That isn't my name. My receptionist would have marked on the envelope that it had been delivered to the wrong person. That private investigator should have done his homework better."

"The investigator was very thorough. Michael is satisfied that you are his daughter. He asked me to bring you back to Virginia Beach to see him. I'd like to do that as soon as possible."

Michele gave him a long, careful look, with the wary scrutiny someone might give a stick of dynamite.

"Just out of curiosity, why in the world would this man's daughter agree to see him when he had ignored her for most of her life? He would be a complete stranger and certainly wouldn't be eligible for Father of the Year, would he?"

"You don't know his side of it."

"You don't know hers."

"Whose?"

"His daughter's."

Through tightly clenched teeth, Cord said, "You are his daughter."

"This conversation is beginning to resemble a poor imitation of Abbott and Costello's comedy baseball routine." He hadn't answered her original question, so she tried again. "Did your partner give you a reason for the length of time it took for him to get around to feeling paternal?"

Her question was similar to the one Cord had asked when Michael had begged him to fetch his daughter. Since he hadn't been given much of an answer, Cord couldn't give her one.

"Michael said there had been complications after the divorce."

"That sounds like an understatement. Or a crock of baloney," she drawled. She came forward in the chair and searched for her shoes with her feet. "I'm sorry you wasted your time and mine, Mr. Thomas, but that's hardly my fault. Your friend's investigator needs to get out his trench coat and spy glass to look under a few more rocks."

He was being dismissed, but she was going to learn it wouldn't be that easy. He had a promise to keep. "I've known Michael Sutherland for ten years. He can be stubborn, opinionated and sometimes a pain in the butt, but I've never known him to lie," he said, his gaze resting on her face.

"Such a paragon, and he's ignored his child since she was two years old. No wonder you think so highly of him," she said dryly. "Do you have any children, Mr. Thomas?"

Cord shook his head.

"Neither do I, but common decency makes his years of neglect hard to accept. You're not going to find it easy to persuade the woman that this man has any rights where she's concerned."

"I'm finding that out."

"Give it up, Mr. Thomas," she said with a small smile. "While I applaud your persistence, you're performing in front of the wrong audience." She clenched her teeth as she pried her sore feet back into the tight shoes. "Lord, I hate these shoes." Putting her palms on the top of the desk, she added, "I hope you find whoever you're looking for, Mr. Thomas, although she has my sympathy. Now if you'll excuse me, I have work to do."

"I was your last appointment. No one else is waiting to see you."

"True, but I do have to check the animals who underwent surgery this morning, and I have other work to take care of before I leave." She stood up, then wished she hadn't. Her feet protested and throbbed painfully. Sitting back in her chair, she removed the shoes again, resisting the urge to toss them into the wastebasket. Going without shoes was the least of her problems at the moment.

She frowned at the man who didn't seem to know a hint when he heard it. He was obviously serious about fulfilling the promise he'd given his partner. Michele could understand his motivation, but not his method.

She could respect his loyalty to his friend, but she wasn't the solution to his problem.

Short of using a tranquilizer gun, she didn't know how she could get him to leave, since he was ignoring her polite dismissal.

In her stocking feet, she stepped around the desk, picking up the stethoscope on her way. If he wouldn't leave, she would.

Cord looked down at her feet, a corner of his mouth twitching when he saw her blue-and-white-striped footwear.

"Nice socks," he drawled.

"Thanks."

"What color would you call that particular shade of blue?"

"Bold blue."

"How about bizarre blue?"

"That, too." For a brief few seconds, her eyes danced with amusement. "My only eccentricity."

"And you keep it hidden from view. It makes me wonder what else you're hiding."

All too soon, her humor faded, to be replaced with a determined glint in her eyes. Cord watched her intently, feeling the same excitement he felt as a child waiting for fireworks to detonate.

Several feet away from him, she stopped. Draping the stethoscope around her neck, she said, "Mr. Thomas, I've been more than patient. I'm not who you think I am and even if I were, I doubt if I would hurry off to meet a man who's known of my existence for over twenty years and has never once tried to see me. I have animals in recovery that need my attention much more than you do."

Cord stood when she started to walk around his chair. He prevented her from leaving the office by stepping in her path.

"Are you really that sure I'm wrong?"

His persistence was really starting to annoy her, and she didn't try to conceal her irritation. "I might not know how to ease world hunger or program my VCR, but I do know my own name and it isn't Sutherland."

"Who told you your father died?"

After a brief hesitation, she answered, "My mother."

Cord watched with interest as she raised her chin defiantly, as though daring him to say anything derogatory about her mother. So he did.

"Why would your mother lie to you about your father's death?"

"I can't think of a single reason," she said tautly.

That statement wasn't entirely true, but she wasn't about to admit that her mother played fast and loose with the truth on a regular basis. Even after all the lies and deceptions she'd put up with from Faith, Michele didn't want to believe Cord Thomas had any basis for his assumption that she was Michael Sutherland's daughter. He was wrong. He had to be. Anything else would mean she'd been living a lie for twenty-six years.

"Why would your partner pretend to have a relationship with me that doesn't exist?" she asked.

"Michael does not lie."

Michele wished she could say the same thing about her mother. "I believe this is what is called a stalemate, Mr. Thomas."

Cord was more than willing to argue the point and opened his mouth to do just that when Michele's gaze shifted to the doorway behind him.

"Did you want me for something, Dixie?" she asked the technician who was standing in the doorway.

Dixie glanced from Michele to Cord, then back to her employer, unabashed curiosity in her gaze. "Sorry to interrupt, but the basset is having a few complications from surgery. I think you'd better look at him."

"I'll be right there." Bringing her gaze back to Cord, Michele said, "I hope your friend's health improves, Mr. Thomas. You obviously care about him a great deal, but I'm not the antidote you're looking for to make him well." She held out her right hand. Smiling faintly, she added, "It's been an interesting experience meeting you."

"Now, or earlier when you were between my legs?"

"Both occasions definitely had their moments," she conceded.

His fingers curled around hers. His callused thumb stroked across the back of her hand for a few seconds. Then he ran a forefinger over her palm as though tracing the lines that would tell her fortune.

"I'll be back," he said quietly. The corners of his mouth curved upward when he felt a shiver of reaction flow through her hand. He would have taken more satisfaction from knowing he could disturb her if he didn't feel a bit shaky himself. "You know that, don't you?"

Michele was unable to ignore the disturbing current radiating from his finger up her arm. But she didn't like it. Puzzled by her reaction to his touch, she met his gaze, hoping she would find some answers in his expression. His gray eyes were dark and unfathomable. His eyes were difficult to read, but the knowing smile curving his hard mouth wasn't. He knew exactly what he was doing, she realized, and he was enjoying himself.

She tried to pull her hand away from his, which only forced him to tighten his hold. "There is no reason for you to come here again, Mr. Thomas. Our business is finished."

His thumb began to stroke over the back of her hand again, his eyes watching her carefully. In a voice soft as silk and as intoxicating as warm brandy, he murmured, "I don't think so. And it's not all business."

Slightly alarmed by the confidence she heard in his voice, Michele tugged at her hand. She was all too aware that he slowly relaxed his grip. The only reason she was free was because he allowed it.

Michele's instincts told her to get as far away from Cord Thomas as possible. If that made her a coward, she could live with that. She stepped around him and walked away. In the doorway, she turned, feeling the need to reinforce the fact she didn't expect to see him again.

"I can't help you with any of your problems, Mr. Thomas. Business or otherwise."

It was the "otherwise" that had his heart rate accelerating. "You mean you won't."

"I mean I can't be anything other than who I am. Mr. Sutherland should ask for a refund from the investigator he hired. He didn't do his job very well. He needs to look somewhere else," she said emphatically.

Then she turned away and walked out of the office with as much dignity as a woman wearing bright striped socks could have.

Cord stared at the doorway even when she was no longer there. He heard her call out to the receptionist that she would be in the surgery and that Gail should leave for the day. A set of footsteps came back down the hall toward the office, but he knew they didn't belong to Michele. This person was wearing rubber-soled shoes, not soft cotton socks.

Dixie appeared in the doorway. "Dr. LaBrock asked me to let you out. The front door is locked because the clinic is closed for the day."

He nodded curtly and followed her to the front door, standing by while she unlocked it for him. She gave him a polite smile as she waited for him to leave. Cord didn't enjoy being treated like an unwelcomed guest, but he wasn't going to do anything about it now.

One thing he'd learned working with boat engines and with businessmen was that timing was extremely important. This wasn't the time to push harder for what he wanted. That would come later.

But not much later. Time was a precious commodity that no one, including Michael's heart specialist, could say he had left.

Chapter Four

After treating the basset hound and checking on the other animals staying overnight for observation, Michele searched through the supply cupboards for a pair of running shoes she'd left at the clinic for the rare occasions when she had some extra time to jog a few miles. She found them tucked away on a back shelf and slipped them on, sighing blissfully at the comfortable fit.

Catching a glimpse of her socks before she crammed her feet into the shoes made her think of Cord Thomas and his amused reaction to her taste in footwear. She would like to forget him and his outrageous request, but she knew that neither would be easy to dismiss from her mind.

From the moment she'd seen him, she'd been thrown off balance by her reaction. As a veterinarian, she was familiar with many components of chemistry. She knew combinations of ingredients that could turn hot or cold and even explode when mixed. This was the first time she'd ever felt the unleashed power of sexual fusion so strongly. And science had nothing to do with it.

His request, which had bordered on a demand, was just as ridiculous. Her mother was not the shrinking violet type. If a man had divorced her, Faith would have added that injustice to the many others on her list that she used as excuses to drink.

Michele didn't shy away from admitting that her own denial had been instinctive. She didn't want to know that her father could have been alive for the past twenty-six years and had chosen to reject her very existence.

And had voluntarily left her with a woman who could barely take care of herself.

A cool breeze had her snapping closed the front of her blue Sand Dune Animal Hospital jacket as she walked toward her car parked in the spacious lot at the back of the building.

Doubt was creeping around the edges of her mind, eating away at her refusal to accept that anything Cord Thomas had told her could be true. As she unlocked her car door, she realized she couldn't simply close her eyes and make Cord Thomas and his bizarre request disappear. Whenever she opened them again, he would be there, as persistent and as stubborn as Willoughby, the Yorkshire terrier who had been responsible for their initial meeting.

Running away from problems never worked. They were always there when you came back. Michele had learned that lesson early. Facing trouble head-on wasn't easy, but it was the only way to fight it.

She slid behind the wheel onto the hot upholstery. The clinic, a small building with a weathered wood exterior, was located two streets from the oceanfront; a large sand dune piled up adjacent to the paved parking space behind the building. Several times a year, Michele had to hire someone to push heaps of sand back toward the dune after the wind scattered a considerable amount onto the parking area. It was a small price to pay for the aesthetic value of having the sand dune preside over her practice.

The ocean breeze and the sand also made it necessary for her to keep her car windows shut during the day except for a narrow space on the driver's side. The interior was like an oven in the summertime, when the temperatures made the mercury rise to the midnineties and above. The sun was still strong and warm in the middle of September, and Michele rolled a window down several inches to let out some of the hot air before turning on the air conditioner.

She didn't immediately drive away. Staring at the dune, she thought how the large mound of sand appeared solid and unchanging. Yet, grain by grain, it was gradually worn down or rearranged by wind and rain, elements of nature that couldn't be predicted or prevented. Looking at the dune made her think of the edgy restlessness that had come over her after the unusual meeting with Cord Thomas. It finally dawned on her that like the sand dune, she was being threatened by outside forces that were beyond her control.

What Cord Thomas had said about her being his partner's daughter was ridiculous. Preposterous. Insane. So why was she even thinking about it? Why was she feeling as though her life was about to be changed irrevocably?

Instead of going home as usual, she turned her compact station wagon in the opposite direction and headed for the two-bedroom cottage she'd bought for her mother four years ago. The few friends Faith LaBrock hadn't completely alienated had made a point of telling Michele that they felt she was treating her mother very badly by making her live alone. Their opinion was based on whatever Faith had decided to tell them. Since her mother enjoyed the role of a martyr, Michele found it easy to imagine the story of neglect Faith would give to whoever would listen. It was probably the same version Faith gave her on occasion.

Michele had followed the advice of the counselors at an alcoholic treatment center by forcing her mother to take responsibility for her own actions. Unable to totally cut off all support, Michele had bought the cottage and paid Faith's living expenses. The change in living arrangements had worked very well for the first year. Then Faith's drinking had steadily escalated again, even though Michele had taken every precaution she could think of to prevent it. She paid for groceries, utilities, clothes—whatever Faith needed—so her mother had no need for cash, which she would invariably use to buy liquor. No matter what preventive measures Michele took, her mother found ways to continue her love affair with alcohol.

With any luck, this would be one of Faith's more coherent days. Michele had some serious questions to ask.

She didn't actually believe Michael Sutherland was her father, but she wanted to have proof when she saw Cord Thomas again. She'd gotten the impression he wasn't the type of man to give up easily. He'd be back. He'd even said so.

In the past, Michele had stayed away from the topic of her father after she'd seen how the subject upset her mother. Michele had learned at an early age how her mother dealt with unpleasant situations. Faith tried repeatedly to drown them in booze.

Michele could only hope that tonight wouldn't be one of those times.

Mrs. Walcott's car was parked in front of the cottage. The third nurse-companion Michele had hired to stay with Faith was lasting longer than the others. So far, a whole month, which was a record. Michele smiled faintly as she thought about how Faith had tried to manipulate the older woman into running errands that would give her time to drink on the sly. Mrs. Walcott had agreed to the idea with one slight change; Faith was to go along. Being exceedingly obnoxious to the woman hadn't worked, either. Nor had pretending to be ill. Faith had met her match. Mrs. Walcott hadn't fallen for any of Faith's tricks. She had lived with an alcoholic husband for twenty years and knew all the clever ruses Faith had perfected to an art form.

Somehow Faith still managed to buy liquor and hide it around the cottage. Neither Michele nor Mrs. Walcott could figure out how she managed to get it into the house in the first place, although they found most of the hiding places she used.

When Michele opened the side door of the cottage, she saw Mrs. Walcott bending over the opened oven door basting several pieces of roasted chicken. Michele waited until the older woman finished what she was doing before she spoke.

After the oven door was closed, Michele said, "That smells good, Mrs. Walcott."

The older woman turned, she was dressed in a cotton floral print housedress, her salt-and-pepper hair disciplined into a tight twist behind her head. Her face was slightly flushed from the heat of the oven and her smile was warm as she greeted Michele.

"It's my grandmother's recipe. Chicken is one of the few things your mother will eat without a lot of persuasion."

Michele smiled. The word *persuasion* covered a lot of ground when it came to dealing with Faith La-Brock. "Is there time for me to talk to her before dinner is ready? There's something I need to discuss with her, and I would like to get it out of the way."

Glancing at the serviceable watch on her thick wrist, Mrs. Walcott said, "The chicken won't be ready for another twenty minutes or so. Your mother is in the front room watching television."

"Thanks. This won't take long." Pausing briefly, she added, "I hope."

As she walked through the kitchen and small dining room, Michele noticed other reasons to appreciate the addition of Mrs. Walcott to the household. Michele had a cleaning company come to the cottage once a week, but Mrs. Walcott disliked dust and clutter and spent a great deal of her time getting rid of both that accumulated in between regular cleanings by the maid service. As much as Michele appreciated Mrs. Walcott's efforts, she didn't want to take advantage of the woman and had protested the extra work she was doing. Taking care of Faith wasn't exactly a time-consuming job, the kind woman had told her. Keeping the house tidy and cooking meals gave her something to do to make her feel she was earning her salary.

Michele passed through the tiny dining alcove and took two steps into the front room. Her footsteps had been muffled by the throw rugs and her rubber-soled shoes, but Michele knew the moment her mother realized she was no longer alone. A slim pint bottle of vodka was quickly stuffed between the cushions of the couch Faith was sitting on. With an automatic smile that contained little pleasure and even less welcome, Faith turned to face her daughter, her cheeks coloring with a guilty flush.

Wearing one of the track suits she favored lately—this one a faded beige—Faith LaBrock no longer resembled the ultrafeminine schoolteacher she'd once been. For convenience rather than style, her grayish blond hair was cropped shorter than most men's. She had once been an attractive woman, full of life and laughter when Michele was a young child. Then, one day, her whole existence began to center around the need for a drink.

Michele had believed the latest doctor's warning about the damage continued alcohol consumption would do to Faith's brain and liver. Faith scoffed at the dire predictions and rejected Michele's numerous attempts to persuade her to quit drinking. The constant tug-of-war created an ongoing tension between the two women.

Faith's voice was slightly husky, her words uttered slowly and occasionally slurred. "Well, my devoted daughter comes to see me after a hard day in puppy-land. To what do I owe this honor?"

Michele ignored the sarcasm that often was directed toward her. She walked over to the end of the couch where her mother was sitting and slid her hand down into the space where Faith had stashed the bottle of vodka. Michele took it with her to a chair opposite the couch and placed it on a small table as she sat down.

Michele didn't bother with a lecture about the vodka. She'd said it all before and her mother had heard it many times in the past. Removing the bottle was a minor victory. They both knew there were others.

Holding her mother's hostile gaze, Michele didn't attempt to make polite conversation. "Something happened today at the clinic that I need to talk to you about."

Placing her hand against her chest in a dramatic gesture, Faith asked, "You need my advice? I don't believe it. Next you'll be telling me there really is a Santa Claus."

Over the years, Michele had learned to read the physical signs that indicated how much liquor her mother had consumed at any given time. The glazed eyes, slurred speech, her level of defensiveness were like gauges of alcohol consumption. Michele could tell Faith wasn't going to be much help to her tonight. Her mother had put away enough vodka to be defiant but not enough to shift her into the gregarious mood that usually followed. This present stage was pure belligerence mixed with sarcasm. It was Michele's least favorite of her mother's moods and the one she faced most often.

Aware of her mother's short attention span, Michele didn't waste any time on detailed explanations. "A man came to the clinic today with a bizarre request for me to go to Virginia Beach to see his partner, who is ill.''

''Unless his partner has four legs and barks, how did he expect you to help his sick partner?''

Michele saw Faith's gaze settle on the bottle on the table and knew she had only half of her attention. ''He was interested in who I was, not what I am.'' Keeping her gaze on her mother's face, she said bluntly, ''He was looking for Michael Sutherland's daughter.''

Faith's eyes widened in horror, her face turning pale under the alcoholic flush. *''What?''*

Her mother's reaction wasn't the one Michele wanted to see. She had hoped for a blank look that would indicate Faith had never heard the name Sutherland before. Obviously her mother knew the name— and the man.

Michele closed her eyes briefly to shut out the shocked expression contorting Faith's face. Raising her lashes, she asked, ''Please tell me he was wrong, Mother.''

''I haven't been able to tell you anything since you turned thirteen, Michele,'' her mother said bitterly. ''You thought you knew it all then, and you still do. It's not an attractive trait.''

Faith stood up, quickly grabbing for the arm of the couch to steady herself when she swayed. ''Your father is dead to us,'' she said harshly. ''That's all I'm going to say on that subject, now or ever. I never want to hear his name again.''

Suddenly feeling ill, Michele watched her mother make her way unsteadily down the hallway to her room. For a few minutes, she didn't move. She could barely even breathe. Her chest felt tight, her breathing constricted. The impact of the final truth had been so staggering, Michele was nearly paralyzed with shock.

"Are you all right, Dr. LaBrock?"

Michele turned to look in the direction of the doorway, where Mrs. Walcott was standing.

She frowned as she considered the older woman's question. Placing her hands on the arms of the chair, she stood slowly, her movements oddly like those of a woman twice her age.

"Not at the moment," she replied to Mrs. Walcott's question. "But I will be."

Concern was etched in Mrs. Walcott's expression and in her voice. "Is there anything I can do?"

Michele shook her head. "Thank you, but this is something I need to deal with myself. I'm sorry you've gone to so much work preparing dinner. You might have to set my mother's dinner aside for a while. I doubt if she'll feel like eating just yet. What I had to ask upset her." She picked up the bottle of vodka and handed it to the older woman. "There are probably others just like this one in her room."

Holding the bottle, Mrs. Walcott stepped aside when Michele approached the doorway. With the insight of a woman accustomed to the mind-set of an alcoholic, she mused aloud. "I'll watch her carefully, Dr. LaBrock. If she's upset, she'll undoubtedly unearth one of her bottles she has stashed away in her bedroom. I won't let her harm herself."

Michelle felt an absurd impulse to be enfolded in the motherly concern emanating from Mrs. Walcott, but she resisted.

"Thank you, Mrs. Walcott. I don't know what I would do without you. If you'll excuse me, I have things I need to do.'' Feeling as though the walls were closing in, she pulled the side door open.

Her guardian angel worked overtime as Michele sped down the outside stairs without any conscious thought about where she was placing her feet. Driven by a primordial desire to flee from the source of her pain, she yanked open her car door and searched frantically in her pocket for her keys. When she drew them out, the keys slipped from her fingers and fell to the sandy, cemented driveway.

Michele stared down at them, noting that her fingers were shaking and ice-cold.

She had enough sense to realize she had no business getting behind the wheel of a car until she was calmer. She bent down to pick up her keys and returned them to the front side pocket of her slacks.

Rather than return to her mother's cottage, Michele left her car where it was and walked toward the ocean a block away. She purposely kept her mind blank until she reached the sandy shore of the Atlantic Ocean. She walked along the beach until she came to a sand dune that the wind had formed in front of a vacant lot. Remnants of the oceanfront house that had once stood on the plot of land behind her served as reminders of the devastation occasionally caused by northeasters and hurricane-force winds.

Michelle sat against the dune and stared out at the gray blue sea. She braced herself mentally for the onslaught of emotions she had to face and deal with.

Her father was alive!

No amount of denial and doubt would change that basic fact. Faith could give excuses and explain her own degree of pain and distress after what Michele reasoned now must have been a divorce. Some of them

might even be valid. But Michele couldn't get past the
fact that her mother had lied, that she was guilty of
gross neglect of the worst kind.

Damn it, she thought, so was the man who was now
claiming a relationship twenty-six years after the fact.
This man, Michael Sutherland, had been aware he had
a daughter all those years, and this was the first time
that he had made an effort to contact her.

Or perhaps he had tried before and Faith had
blocked any communication from him. Michele could
imagine her mother doing such a thing.

At the moment, she didn't know the truth from a
fabrication wrapped up in pretty words and promises.

So much of her life had been a lie, and now she had
another one to add to the long list. She had made numerous excuses for her mother over the years; when
Michele encountered parents of some of the children
Faith had taught in school, she'd say Faith was enjoying retirement. That had been a lie. As a teenager,
she'd pretended her mother had other social commit-
ments that prevented her from attending the plays
Michele had performed in. Another lie. She'd agreed
with people who commented on the selfless dedica-
tion of her mother raising a daughter alone. A major
lie.

She'd hidden the truth so long, Michele wasn't sure
she even knew what it was anymore. She'd better sort
out the facts from the falsehoods before she saw Cord
Thomas again, she told herself. He hadn't impressed
her as the type of man to be put off by half-truths or
flimsy excuses. Nor did he seem the type of man to
give up easily when he wanted something.

Cord Thomas was a complication she could have done without, even if he hadn't been the catalyst for turning her life upside down and sideways. Her reaction to him personally had nothing to do with his reason for coming to see her and made the situation even more confusing than it was already.

The pager she wore on her belt signaled that someone was trying to reach her. She started walking back to her car quickly, relieved to have work to think about rather than dwelling on the sharp turn her life had suddenly taken.

Later that evening, she arrived home after taking care of an emergency at the clinic. She'd had time to kick off her shoes and fix a cup of tea when the phone rang a little after nine. She picked up the extension in her bedroom where she'd gone to change into her nightgown and robe.

She recognized Cord's voice when he immediately demanded, "Meet me someplace for a drink."

She could have pretended she didn't know who it was, but she didn't bother. "Please say this is an obscene phone call, Mr. Thomas, so I can hang up."

"Sorry," he said after chuckling briefly. "This is the real thing. Men have been plying women with fermented beverages for centuries. I thought I'd try it with you."

Michele tucked the phone into the crook of her neck so she could finish buttoning the front of her nightgown.

"I don't drink," she replied, leaving out the reasons behind her abstinence from anything stronger than a glass of lemonade.

"Not even a glass of water?"

"Water I drink. Liquor I don't."

"Never or only with me?"

Feeling inexplicably better now that she was adequately covered, she held the receiver in her hand.

"Never," she answered.

"Well, meet me someplace for a cup of coffee, then."

She smiled. "Caffeine at this hour? I'd be awake all night."

The tone of his voice changed. "That's okay with me."

Her smile disappeared. She placed her free hand on her stomach, which suddenly felt strange. "If you're bored, why don't you read a good book or watch television?" she asked.

"It's not quite the same thing," he drawled lazily.

"Where are you?" she asked cautiously. She wouldn't be surprised if he was parked in front of her cottage, calling her on a mobile phone.

He named a local hotel and even furnished the room number. "The brochure the maid left brags about the hotel's efficient room service. Want to try it out with me?"

Michele felt a sliver of panic. She was actually tempted! She sank down onto the edge of the mattress, but that made her think of the bed in his hotel room, so she quickly stood again, feeling foolish.

"I haven't changed my mind about seeing Mr. Sutherland," she said with more confidence than she felt.

"I didn't think you had." He paused for a few seconds, then said, "Damn it, Michele, I want to see you."

Her stomach did flip-flops again. "Cord..."

She had no way of knowing what the sound of his name said with that sighing catch in her voice did to him. Or that he sensed her vulnerability.

"All right. Not tonight." He took a deep breath and said gently, "This trip to Nags Head hasn't turned out the way I expected since I looked down and found you between my legs."

"You make it sound more personal than it was."

"It felt damn personal to me at the time."

Michele watched her tan-and-white cat, Coco, daintily walk across the bed as though treading on eggs. Michele had the same feeling about her conversation with Cord.

"Cord," she began hesitantly. "I don't want you to get the wrong impression. There can't be anything between us."

"Why not?"

The casual way he phrased the question made her wonder if he had any idea of the upheaval he'd caused in her life.

"Did you ever hear the saying about shooting the messenger when the news he'd brought hadn't been what the person wanted to hear?"

After a brief silence, Cord said, "There's another saying that you can't fight Mother Nature. That applies to the natural forces between men and women, too. I don't plan on fighting what feels right. Think about that. Good night, Michele. Sleep well."

"You, too," she managed. "Good night."

She heard the click indicating he'd hung up. She slowly replaced the receiver and sat down on the edge of the bed. Coco sidled up to Michele's side and pressed against her. Michele idly scratched the cat's ears.

She had never felt less like sleeping in her whole life.

Chapter Five

The following morning, Michele kept busy during several hours of surgery. Along with routine neutering and spaying operations, she'd removed a post office box key swallowed by a golden Labrador retriever much to the relief of the dog's owner, who ran a lucrative mail-order business. Luckily, neither the key nor the dog were seriously damaged by the experience.

The work load in the clinic was lightened by the presence of Michele's partner, Bud Jameson, who had returned from his honeymoon. The drawback to having Bud back at the clinic was having to listen to his ecstatic descriptions of his new role as a bridegroom. No detail was too small to mention, no remark made by his bride too mundane to repeat. Michele's endurance was stretched to the limit by noon.

So was her imagination. She hadn't seen any examples of wedded bliss to make her believe in such a thing as the happy-ever-after Bud described. Since Michele didn't want to dampen his enthusiasm, she pasted a smile on her face and said the appropriate words when necessary.

Luckily, the pictures Bud and his bride had taken during their honeymoon trip to the Caribbean hadn't been developed yet, so Michele could postpone trying to think of adjectives to describe each and every photograph.

She ate lunch with Bud in the back room, where the staff usually took their breaks, and she said all the suitable things to a newlywed who was an enthusiastic advocate of the marital state after surviving for fifteen straight days and nights without even a hint of discord.

"You should take the plunge one of these days, Michele," he droned for about the fifth time since his return. "Being married is really great. Having someone to come home to makes all the difference at the end of a day."

She smiled. "So you've said several times. You now eat home-cooked meals on real plates instead of out of cardboard containers. Your clothes magically disappear from the floor and return clean to your dresser drawers and closets, and you no longer have to hunt for your car keys because Rita knows exactly where they are at all times. I'll break this to you as gently as I can, Bud. Most women do those things for themselves. A wedding ring isn't mandatory."

Grinning, Bud said, "I could mention a few other benefits of married life, but I don't want to offend your fragile sensibilities."

"I appreciate that," she said dryly as she brushed crumbs off the table. "I shock so easily."

"Sure you do," he drawled lazily. "This from a woman who didn't blink an eye when she extracted a pair of lacy bikini briefs swallowed by the preacher's cat."

Michele grinned.

Bud started to add more to his liturgy on marriage when Dixie interrupted by sticking her head through the doorway. "That good-looking guy with no appointment is back again, Dr. LaBrock. Gail says he insists on seeing you right away."

Even though she'd been expecting Cord to appear again, Michele felt the muscles in her stomach knot with tension. It was a frail hope it would work, but she made a suggestion. "Tell him to make an appointment like everyone else."

Whatever Dixie meant to say became a garbled sound of surprise when she was bodily moved out of the way, replaced in the doorway by the tall lean figure of Cord Thomas. Dressed in jeans and a black cotton shirt, he looked dark, dangerous and determined.

Michele leaned against the back of the metal folding chair and crossed her arms over her chest. She saw Cord's gray eyes shift from her to Bud, then return to meet her cool gaze.

"We need to talk now, Michele," he said quietly. "Not later."

Bud's curiosity broke the silence that followed. Glancing at Michele's closed expression, he commented, "It looks like you left a few things out of the report you gave me about what's been going on around here while I've been gone."

Cord's dark gaze shifted to Bud. "Who the hell are you?"

Instead of being offended, Bud was clearly amused. He rearranged his long legs so he could stand without toppling the chair. Smiling broadly, he extended his right hand. "Bud Jameson, D.V.M., Doctor of Veterinarian Medicine, in case you aren't familiar with the initials. I'm Michele's partner, a recent bridegroom and one hell of a nice guy. And you are?"

"Leaving," Michele interjected hopefully.

Cord stepped forward and clasped Bud's hand, slanting a half smile in Michele's direction. "Cord Thomas, marina owner from Virginia Beach, not particularly nice and I need to talk to Michele. Alone."

Releasing Cord's hand, Bud removed his blue Sand Dune jacket from the back of his chair. "I don't see where that's a problem. I'll take your next two appointments, Michele. That will give you twenty minutes or so to have your chat with Mr. Thomas."

Michele opened her mouth to protest, but Bud's long legs had already carried him out of the small lunchroom. She looked at Cord. "You have a lot in common with your partner in the stubborn department, Mr. Thomas."

"We can dispense with the formalities, Michele. You called me Cord last night. Why does everyone else wear those jackets around here but you?"

She had no idea what the jackets had to do with anything, but she answered him anyway. "I do wear one if I know I'm going to be dealing with a frightened or vicious animal. The tough material protects our arms from most scratches and bites."

Standing beside her chair, Cord reached for her hand, running the tips of his fingers over the scar he found on the inside of her forearm below the short sleeve of her shirt. His stomach clenched. He didn't like the idea of an animal's claws or teeth tearing her soft skin.

"Is this scar from an animal bite?"

She nodded. "It comes with the territory. I've only been in the hospital once in four years, with an infection from a bite from a cat, so I've been lucky."

"Lucky? You call being bitten lucky?"

"It's usually due to my own carelessness." She drew her arm away from his hands. "If that was all you wanted to know, I'll go help Bud with the office calls."

He ignored her attempt to get rid of him. "Did you talk to your mother about Michael Sutherland?"

"Yes."

His gray eyes never left her face, his gaze sharply intent on the defensive tilt of her chin. Cord had seen that same expression on her face before. And for the same reason. He'd mentioned her mother. Interesting, he thought. And a curious reaction. He'd skimmed over the investigator's report on Michele's mother. Now he wished he'd paid more attention.

"Did your mother confirm or deny that Michael Sutherland is your father?"

Michele concentrated on folding the plastic wrapper from her sandwich. "She repeated what she told me years ago. She insists my father is dead."

Cord would like to have had more privacy than the lunchroom provided, but he would settle for these few minutes with her if this was all he was going to get. Taking the chair across from her, he reached into the back pocket of his jeans and withdrew an envelope. He held it out to her.

She looked at it but didn't take it. "What's that?"

"Open it and read what it says."

"Why?"

He sighed heavily. "Shouting at Michael usually works when he is being pigheaded. I'll use the same procedure on you if necessary." His gaze flicked briefly to the envelope. "Do us both a favor, Michele. Read the paper."

She stared at the envelope. She had a strange feeling that once she read the contents, her life would never be the same. She knew she could delay opening the envelope now, and maybe even the next time, but she also knew that Cord would keep badgering her until she looked at whatever was in the envelope.

Placing the tip of her finger on the envelope, she slowly slid it across the table toward her. The envelope was blank on the outside and lightly sealed. She picked it up and slipped a fingernail under the glued flap. Then she withdrew several sheets of paper and unfolded them.

It was a faxed copy of a divorce decree.

Michele silently read the names on the legal document that ended a marriage between Faith Laraine LaBrock Sutherland and Michael Neal Sutherland. Custody of their daughter, Michele Diana Sutherland, was given to the mother with unlimited visitation rights allowed to the father. The date of the divorce was twenty-six years ago, the same year Michele had been told her father had supposedly died. She would have been two years old.

This was irrevocable proof her father had been very much alive when he'd left them. Faith had evidently considered death preferable to divorce in explaining his absence from their lives. Her mother had never been a great fan of the truth, Michele mused, but lying about her husband's death was monstrous even for her. Michele glanced over the paper again, reading the name of Michael Sutherland. In a different way, the man listed as her father had been just as cruel and thoughtless. Michele hadn't known of his existence, but he had known about hers. And had voluntarily stayed out of her life for twenty-six years.

She couldn't get past that simple fact, or forgive his neglect just because he was ready to see her now. It was too late—twenty-six years too late.

"Michele?"

When she looked up, Cord was staring at her with a strange expression. "What?"

Cord didn't like the frozen look on her face. Or the flat tone of her voice. "Don't you have anything to say about the proof that Michael Sutherland is your father?"

"I can't think of a thing," she said politely. She folded the paper and slid it back into the envelope. Holding it out to him, she said, "Would you like this back or am I supposed to keep it on file?"

"When you refused to believe what I told you about your relationship with Michael, I had his secretary fax a copy of the divorce papers for you to see. File them, tear them up, burn them. I really don't give a damn what you do with them." He was angry without knowing why. "As long as you believe what it says, that Michael Sutherland is your father and has a right to see you before he dies, they've served their purpose."

"The document states he was married to my mother and that they were divorced." She stood, leaving the envelope on the table among the sandwich wrappers and other luncheon debris. "I noticed it also gave him unlimited visitation rights to see his daughter. That appears to be me. Since I don't remember him, he obviously never took advantage of that option, so don't tell me he has any rights where I'm concerned."

"Aren't you even curious about the man who is your father?" Cord asked in disbelief.

"Leave me with a few illusions," she stated with a cutting sarcasm. "I didn't blame my father for leaving me alone when I thought he had died. Knowing he chose to stay out of my life of his own free will is hard enough to accept without learning why. I doubt if I'll care much more for his reason than I do for his lack of interest during the last twenty-six years."

"You aren't being fair to him, Michele."

"Probably not," she admitted. "I don't feel particularly charitable toward the man right now."

Cord couldn't entirely blame her for feeling that way. Abandonment came in a variety of forms. He had often thought of what he would do or say if his mother walked back into his life. His responses had changed over the years as the distance of time made the past fade.

But the devastation of knowing his mother hadn't loved him had never been completely erased from his memory.

"At least hear his side of the story, Michele. I know Michael. He had to have had a damn good reason for staying out of your life as he apparently has. He's a decent, caring man. All I'm asking is for you to give him a chance to explain what happened between him and your mother.''

The mention of her mother made Michele hesitate to give Cord a flat refusal. He felt he knew his partner well and was willing to give him the benefit of the doubt. She, on the other hand, knew her mother's regular abuse of the truth.

''Your partner has known he's had a daughter for twenty-eight years,'' she stated. ''I just found out about him. I'd like a little time to take it all in.''

''He might not have a lot of time left,'' Cord said quietly.

She gave him a quelling glance. ''Don't try to put a guilt trip on me, Mr. Thomas. I'm the one who didn't know about him, not the other way around.''

Before Cord could stop her, Michele stepped around her chair and left the lunchroom. He looked down at the envelope, which he had mistakenly thought would solve his problem.

He had accomplished one goal. She now believed that Michael Sutherland was her father. Unfortunately, the document also proved that Michael hadn't given a damn about her for most of her life.

Cord couldn't blame her for resenting being neglected by a parent. Hell, he was an expert on how it felt to be abandoned and forgotten. He could understand how Michele was feeling, but he had made a promise to Michael, and he didn't break promises.

But he also didn't like knowing he had been the person responsible for hurting Michele. He didn't want to feel guilty. Damn it, he didn't want to feel anything at all!

His defenses had been breached by a green-eyed lady vet much too easily, he realized without understanding how. Before he saw her again, he would have to shore up the invisible barrier he erected around himself to avoid getting personally involved in someone else's life.

He picked up the envelope he'd brought with him and tore it in two before dropping it into a trash bin. For a few minutes, he stared down at the innocuous scraps of paper, wondering why the hollow feeling he had carried around deep inside him for as long as he could remember seemed to have grown, the emptiness a dark cavern pulling him down into a vacant nothingness. The gaping hole was as familiar to him as the face he shaved every morning.

But it had never hurt before. It was just there, a permanent part of him since the day he understood his mother wasn't coming back for him. So why was he feeling raw and cold and lost all over again?

A ragged piece of paper that had slipped out of the torn envelope caught his eye. He bent down and picked up the fragment of the legal document, which had the typed name of Michele Diana Sutherland on it.

He ran the pad of his forefinger across her name and thought of her amused green eyes looking up at him after she'd caught the runaway Yorkshire terrier. He felt a surge of heat pushing away some of the chill from his soul.

For a moment, he simply absorbed the sensation until it settled deep inside him like a reassuring ring of warmth. He no longer wondered about the source of the strange feeling. He didn't know how or why, but he knew who was responsible for bringing him back to life. Michele.

Now he had another reason for wanting her to go to Virginia Beach.

Chapter Six

Cord had planned his arrival at the animal hospital that afternoon to coincide with its scheduled closing time. After two frustrating hours on the phone arranging for a sump pump to be delivered and installed on one of his charter boats, he wasn't in the mood to sit in Michele's cubbyhole office again until she got around to talking to him.

His brief conversation with his partner hadn't done much to improve Cord's mood, either, since he hadn't been able to tell Michael what he wanted to hear. He couldn't give him a definite date or even any hope that Michele would arrive in Virginia Beach at all. Hearing the hunger in Michael's voice when he asked Cord to tell him what his daughter was like made Cord more determined than ever to somehow get Michele and her father together.

Remembering Michele's reaction to the divorce document as he drove to her clinic, Cord didn't expect her to roll out the welcome mat for him this time, either. It was more likely that she would throw him out of the place.

It had taken Cord a while to realize that his odd, restless mood all afternoon had to do with his anticipation of seeing Michele again. The knowledge that he had hurt her, albeit unintentionally, bothered the hell out of him. He needed to make peace with her before he could find it for himself.

This time he wasn't as overconfident as he'd been before the previous two meetings. Planning his approach was a waste of time. Michele hadn't reacted the way he'd expected at their first confrontation, and the second had been a disaster. He didn't fool himself into thinking this meeting would go any smoother.

Her reaction to seeing the divorce papers puzzled him. He wasn't sure exactly how he would have reacted under the same circumstances, but the way she'd withdrawn inside herself had been frustrating. It was as though she'd pulled a curtain down over her emotions, effectively shutting him out. His ex-wife had used tears and her body as weapons during any disagreement they had. His partner staged long-winded speeches to wear down his opponent. Before he died, Rocky had used every cuss word he'd learned in seventy-five years whenever he was angry. Cord hadn't the faintest idea how to combat Michele's silence.

When he was about to turn into the driveway of the clinic, a small white station wagon was on its way out. He didn't pay much attention to it other than waiting for the car to get out of his way. But he caught a glimpse of blond hair and looked closer. Michele pulled out in front of him onto the road during a break in traffic.

A car behind him honked impatiently when Cord changed his mind about turning off and drove straight ahead instead. He had no way of knowing where Michele was going, but he knew her destination wasn't her home. That afternoon, he'd checked out the address the investigator had included in his report and her cottage was in the opposite direction.

She was leading him on a merry chase in more ways than this one, he admitted. And he was letting her. That fact alone should tell him something about the extent of his interest in her. There were a hundred reasons why he shouldn't get involved with her other than that she was Michael's daughter.

And only one reason to explain his odd preoccupation: he wanted her.

Oddly enough, it wasn't only a physical attraction that was drawing him toward her. It was something else, some nebulous thing as yet unidentified in his mind. He recognized the need to see her, to talk to her and to touch her. Lord, did he want to touch her. Maybe then he would find the answer to this mysterious longing gnawing in his gut.

Last night Cord had stared at the ceiling in his hotel room and had admitted to himself that he could have handled the initial meeting with Michele better than he had. He should have approached the subject of her father with a bit more tact instead of bludgeoning her over the head with Michael's request to see her. Before he'd met Michele, Cord had found it easier to think of her as a cold, neglectful daughter who had shut her father out of her life. Cord's attitude initially had reflected his ambivalent feelings, he'd admitted to himself.

Their second meeting at noon hadn't gone much better, and he took the blame for that, too, although he couldn't have known her reaction to the proof of her true identity would be so extreme.

It shouldn't matter so much that he'd hurt her by telling her the truth. But it did matter.

Because she mattered.

Up ahead, she turned her car into a side street, and Cord followed a few moments later. Looking around, he saw that they were in a section of the seaside town that was made up of cottages built mostly on pilings because of their proximity to the ocean, with its high tides and turbulent surf. The majority of dwellings had the living quarters on the second floor, with parking and storage below between the pilings. This thin strip of land called the Outer Banks was vulnerable to powerful storms and violent hurricanes, but people kept building more houses every year anyway.

Cord wondered which of the houses was Michele's destination. He soon found out. Halfway down the block, she slowed and turned into a driveway, parking behind an older-model car badly in need of a paint job.

Cord pulled over to the side of the road near the corner and watched through the windshield as Michele got out of her car. His gaze followed her as she took the stairs up to a door located on the right side of the cottage. Cord waited to see if a man came to the door. Considering his own reaction to her, he found it easy to assume that Michele would be involved with someone.

What was unreasonable was the extent of his anger at the thought of her being with another man.

From where he was parked, Cord could see the gray-haired woman who opened the door. Relief washed through him. He had no way of knowing what Michele or the other woman he assumed was her mother were saying, but he observed that Michele didn't appear to like what she was hearing. As he watched, she slumped wearily against the side of the railing and stared down at the step she was standing on while she listened.

Cord thought it was odd that Michele didn't go inside. From what he could tell by their actions, neither woman was expecting to carry on a lengthy discussion.

Finally, Michele agreed to something the other woman said by nodding before turning abruptly to go back down the steps. The woman near the door watched Michele for a few seconds, then went back into the cottage and shut the door. Cord watched Michele return to her car. He closed his fingers around the ignition key so he could trail after her again when she drove off.

Except she didn't go anywhere.

The late-afternoon sun was glaring off the glass of the station wagon's rear window, and it was impossible for Cord to see what Michele was doing inside her car. She certainly wasn't starting the engine.

Puzzled and a little concerned, Cord pushed open his door. Keeping his gaze on her car, he stepped out onto the blacktopped road. Gritty sand on the road crunched under his shoes as he approached her car from behind.

When he finally did see her, he quickened his step. Her arms were crossed over the top of the steering wheel, and she was resting her forehead on the back of one of her wrists.

Yanking open the door, Cord placed his hand on her shoulder, his fingers squeezing several times. "Michele? This is a hell of a time to take a nap. Wake up."

Michele had needed just a few minutes to gather her thoughts, but she wasn't going to be allowed that luxury. She certainly didn't need another confrontation with Cord Thomas right now. But her childhood had made her an expert on accepting things she couldn't do anything about, so she took a deep breath and slowly raised her head.

Meeting Cord's frowning gaze, she said without rancor, "I was just wondering what else could possibly happen to make today one of the all-time worst days this month, and here you are."

"It's nice to know I serve a purpose." It took only one glance for Cord to see the world-weary expression in the depths of her haunting green eyes. He suspected the cause was from more than a typical bad day.

"What's wrong?" he asked quietly.

She straightened up behind the wheel. Answering his question with one of her own, she asked, "Have you been following me?"

"Damn right."

"Harass somebody else for a change. I'm not in the mood."

"Invite me along, then I won't have to resort to trailing after you." Cord straightened, leaning an arm on the top of the open car door. Glancing briefly at the cottage, he brought his gaze back to hers. "Your visit didn't last very long."

"Long enough," she murmured. Smiling faintly, she asked, "Would you believe I was making a house call?"

"No."

She shrugged. "It was worth a try."

"It might have worked if the woman who came to the door had been holding a cat or a dog or if you had taken that official-looking leather case in the back seat."

She glared at him. "What are you? Some sort of apprentice Peeping Tom?"

"I was waiting for you to finish your little chat at the top of the stairs. Then you and I were going to have a big chat. I was on my way to the clinic to see you when you left. We still have a few minor subjects to cover, and I want to get them out of the way." He saw the shadows return to her eyes a few seconds before she looked away. "We might not be friends yet, Michele," he added gravely. "But I'm not your enemy."

Her ghost of a smile vaguely resembled the real thing. "I know."

"Then stop treating me like one. The next couple of days will go a lot smoother for both of us if you do."

"I wish you would believe me when I tell you I can't go to Virginia Beach. I'm not saying I won't eventually go to meet Michael Sutherland—"

"Your father," he persisted.

"I know who he is."

"You can deny it all you want, but it's true and you know it now."

"You are really beginning to annoy me, Mr. Thomas. That's not a healthy thing to do to a person who knows how to operate a tranquilizer gun that could bring down a bull elephant."

"I'll take my chances." With relief, he realized she was protesting only for the sake of protesting. Humor laced her voice. But her eyes were still haunted. "Tell me why you're upset."

Her teeth were clenched slightly in an exaggerated grimace when she answered, "I'm not upset. See, I'm smiling."

He wasn't buying what she was trying to sell. "Your father would want me to help you if you were having some kind of problem, Michele. Just tell me what's bothering you, and we'll go on from there."

She glanced at the cottage in front of her. "You really don't know who lives here, do you?"

"Why would I be asking if I already knew?" His earlier assumption might not have been right. Lord knows, he'd been wrong several times during the past twenty-four hours.

"Who knows? You've done several things the last couple of days that I haven't understood. Why would this time be any different?"

"It just is. Why are you upset?"

"And here I thought you were a man who knew all the answers."

"Michele," he warned.

She relented. "If you ever need the services of a private investigator, I suggest you don't use the one your partner hired. This is where my mother, Faith LaBrock, lives. I suppose, to be technically correct, I should say Faith LaBrock Sutherland. The investigator should have known her address. She was mentioned quite prominently in the divorce decree, if you remember.''

"I remember." Damn it, he thought. That wounded doe expression was back in her eyes again. "Apparently, she isn't any more thrilled with my visit to Nags Head than you are." When Michele gave him a blank look, he added, "I saw you shaking your head at something she said while you were talking to her. Or I should say when she was talking to you. I assumed you told her I was still hounding you, and she didn't like it any better than you do."

"The woman who came to the door is Mrs. Walcott." Her puzzled expression disappeared. "She stays with my mother. Somehow Faith slipped by her about an hour ago and is out on the town."

Cord thought the phrasing Michele used for her mother leaving the cottage was odd. "Is your mother ill?"

She shook her head slowly. "Not the way you mean."

"In what way, then? Why are you and the other woman disturbed because your mother isn't home?"

A lifetime of hiding Faith's drinking was impossible to overcome that easily. She waved his question aside. "It doesn't matter."

"Of course it matters, if what she's doing is upsetting you. Does her leaving the cottage have anything to do with my visit? You said earlier that you had asked her about your father, and she denied that he was alive. I'd hate to think I've caused problems for you with your mother."

"My mother has some health problems," she said evasively. "I was sitting here debating whether or not to go looking for her. It's not easy for me to ignore the possibility that she might hurt herself.''

"Move over," he ordered as he came away from the door and waited for her to make room for him to slide behind the wheel. "I'll go with you. I probably should talk to her about Michael, anyway.''

"No. You shouldn't," she said with a ghost of a laugh. "Talking to her about him last night is the excuse she'll use when I catch up with her.''

"We're wasting time, Michele. I'm going with you.''

Michele's first instinct was to refuse, so Cord wouldn't see her mother in a drunken state. That was the code of the child of an alcoholic, to keep the secret, to pretend everything was normal. Considering Cord already knew more about her personal life than anyone else on the face of the earth, Michele decided it wasn't necessary to hide her mother's drinking from him.

Plus, she realized that taking him along might accomplish what she hadn't been able to do so far and that was to convince him to return to Virginia Beach without her. He wouldn't be the first person to be turned off by the sight of her mother after she'd been drinking.

"Get in, then," she ordered. "But I'll drive.''

Cord didn't wait for a friendlier invitation. His long strides ate up the ground as he walked around the station wagon to the passenger side. He slid onto the seat and automatically reached for the seat belt.

Michele didn't start the engine immediately. "We need to agree on some rules before we go anywhere. You can't interfere when I find my mother. You have to promise to stay out of whatever we run into, or you can't go with me.''

"How can I promise that when I don't know what's ahead of us?"

"Very easily. By saying you'll let me handle things my way."

Cord rarely walked into any situation without knowing exactly what he was doing or where he was going and why. She was asking him to go against one of his own rules. Yet he didn't want her to be alone when she drove around Nags Head looking for her mother. He had no idea why he felt so protective toward her. She hadn't shown the slightest tendency to shy away from fighting her own battles.

"All right," he agreed reluctantly. "I'll stay in the background under one condition."

"No conditions," she said adamantly. "That's not part of the deal."

"You didn't let me finish. If we encounter any type of situation where I feel you're in danger, I'm going to do something about it whether I have your permission or not."

"I've done this before," she commented as she leaned forward to turn the key in the ignition. "I know what I'm doing, and I doubt very much if you do."

Cord frowned at her cryptic remark, puzzling over it. "How do you know where to look? She could have gone anywhere."

"She can't go too far. She doesn't have a license or a car. The police took away the license, and I took the car."

She had been right about the investigator slipping up about information concerning her mother, Cord speculated. There hadn't been anything in the part of the report he'd read about Faith Labrock being ill enough to require someone to live with her or having a tendency to take off on little jaunts that caused Michele to look for her. All he remembered from the report was that Michele's mother had taught school when Michele was younger but was now retired and dependent on her daughter.

Cord had no idea what was wrong with Michele's mother, but he had the feeling that after tonight he would know.

Michele drove for about ten minutes before pulling into the parking lot of a large beachfront hotel. "I won't be long. I doubt if she's here, but I need to check it out since this place is closest to her cottage."

His hand went to the door. "*We'll* check it out," he corrected.

Michele gave him an impatient glance but didn't object when he opened his door.

She didn't go into the hotel's front entrance to check with the registration desk as Cord had expected. Instead she walked to a separate doorway, to a restaurant/bar located in part of the hotel.

Cord stayed just inside the entrance as Michele walked up to the bar, where the bartender was grinning at something one of his customers was saying, until he saw Michele. The smile was replaced by a grimace as he slowly walked to her end of the bar with as much enthusiasm as if he was on his way to his own hanging. This scene had obviously been played out before, Cord realized.

Cord couldn't hear what Michele asked him, but he could see the negative shake of the bartender's head. Then Michele nodded abruptly and turned away. After glancing around at the patrons sitting at tables and in booths, she brushed past Cord without a comment or an explanation and returned to the car.

For the next thirty minutes, Michele followed basically the same procedure at various other places. They would park, go in, she would question the bartender or a waitress who all seemed to know what she was going to ask. Then, after a quick look around, Michele would return to the car and drive to the next location.

Cord didn't like the looks of the bar that was next on their route. One of the small windows in front that had been painted black had a wide strip of silver duct tape over a crack in the glass. Three light bulbs were broken in the sign extending upward from the roof. A junked car was parked near the door, two wheels missing and several side windows broken. Several motorcycles in less than pristine condition were parked side by side.

The inside wasn't much better. A haze of cigarette smoke made it difficult to see much more than four feet in front of them. The noise level was uncomfortably loud. A jukebox and fifty or so patrons all talking at once competed with the clatter of glassware and chairs scraping on the grimy parquet floor.

Following her usual pattern, Michele approached the bar after glancing around at the occupants of the tables and booths.

The chat with the bartender didn't follow the routine this time. His expression was similar to most of the others she'd questioned that night, Cord noticed. This one wasn't any happier to see her than the others had been. That was where the similarity to previous encounters ended.

When the bartender nodded and drew something out of his pocket to show her, Michele grabbed the front of the man's black shirt, exerting enough force to bring him partially over the counter. That was enough to make Cord break his promise about not interfering.

When he stepped forward, Cord heard Michele say, "You promised you wouldn't take anything in trade from her again, Harry."

"She's not an easy lady to turn down, Mick. She started crying, damn it. I can take a lot of things but seeing one of my schoolteachers crying ain't one of 'em."

"You gave your word, Harry. I thought that was still worth something."

Cord didn't wait for the bartender's answer. He saw what Michele didn't see, and that was two large burly men scowling at her as they left their bar stools and started walking toward her end of the bar. Cord reached around Michele to grab her wrist to break her hold on the front of the bartender's shirt.

She jerked her head around and glared at Cord. "Now *you* break your promise. You weren't supposed to interfere, remember?"

"I'm just evening up the odds a little in your favor," he murmured close to her ear. "Look to your right."

Michele shifted her gaze to include the two large men who had stopped two feet away with fists like hams clamped to their hips.

She shrugged them off as though they were two pesky flies she could easily squash, and the look in her eyes implied she would relish doing exactly that. "I've about had it with men this evening, gentlemen, so don't come any closer. You'll regret it if you do."

Cord nearly groaned aloud. The idiot woman was daring the two men and didn't even realize it. Now they had to step in'. Their male code of the truly machismo would demand satisfaction.

"Michele, shut up," warned Cord under his breath.

The two men took a step toward Michele. One of them said, "You got quite a mouth on you, lady. Someone should teach you some manners."

"You have to know some before you can teach them," she said rudely. Turning back to the bartender, she asked, "How much did you give Faith for the watch, Harry?"

He gave her a figure, a pitifully small amount that added fuel to the fire of anger burning inside Michele. She reached into a pocket of her slacks and took out a bundle of folded money. Peeling off the amount Harry had given Faith, she laid the cash on the bar and picked up the watch.

"This has to be the last time, Harry. You aren't helping Faith by letting her hock her possessions for drinks."

The bartender held up his hand palm out. "I won't do it again, Mickie. I swear."

"I've heard that before, and look what happened," she scoffed. "Your promise is as weak as your drinks."

One of the large bystanders took exception to her less than respectful attitude. His first mistake was saying so. "You need to be taught some respect for menfolk, missy."

His second error came when he grabbed her wrist.

She waited until he stepped closer before she suddenly turned and used the man's grip on her wrist, along with his forward momentum, as leverage to swing him around to collide into the other man.

Both men were knocked off their feet, and they ended up in a pile on the floor between the bar and a table occupied with patrons, who jumped to their feet in order to get out of the way. To add to the confusion, a vacant chair toppled down in front of Cord, and he tripped over it as he stepped toward Michele with the intention of getting her the hell out of there. The next few minutes were filled with a great deal of colorful curses as the three men untangled themselves from the chair and one another.

By the time Cord was back on his feet again, Michele was gone.

As only men can, Cord initiated peace by buying both of the men a beer, and the disagreement was forgotten as everybody suddenly became buddies.

As he was paying the bartender, Cord said, "From what I heard of your conversation with Michele, you evidently know her pretty well."

"No one knows Mickie very well," mumbled Harry as he tried to smooth down the wrinkled front of his shirt. "I think she prefers it that way."

"Mickie?"

The bartender smiled faintly. "That was her nickname in high school. She hates it, but it's automatic with me."

"You went to school with Michele?" When Harry nodded, Cord slid onto one of the barstools. "Tell me what you know about her and her mother."

Chapter Seven

Sitting in a booth at the fast-food restaurant across the street from the bar, Michele stared at her hands cupped around a steaming mug of coffee. Amazingly enough, they were steady, even though her stomach was still doing a tap dance. She hated scenes, but she'd just been responsible for starting one. And she had involved Cord Thomas, her father's friend and partner.

The report Cord gave Michael Sutherland would undoubtedly cover the events in the bar and her part in the ruckus. Having a daughter involved in a barroom brawl might be more than her father had bargained for when he sent Cord to Nags Head.

It had been stupid to go through the ritual of searching for Faith in the first place, she admitted. In the past, she'd never accomplished anything except to make Faith angry and leave herself feeling demoralized. After the last time, Michele had sworn she wouldn't tramp through bars looking for her mother again.

So why had she felt the necessity to put herself through that again tonight? she wondered. Was she trying to play that childish game where she could make things right if she could only get Faith home?

Or did learning about her father's neglect make her want to prove that at least one parent needed her?

The questions came easily, but the answers remained elusive.

She glanced up when she heard someone slide onto the imitation leather seat on the other side of the table.

"Feel better?" Cord asked casually.

She shook her head. "Not particularly," she murmured with a faint, self-mocking smile.

Cord looked down at the cup of hot coffee on the table in front of him. "It looks like you were expecting me."

"I knew you would turn up. All you had to do was see my car parked across the street from the bar and see me sitting in the booth by the window. I knew you would come, if only for a ride back to your car. How many beers did you have to buy to calm down the brawn brothers?"

A corner of his mouth twitched. "Two each, and I had to listen to a stern lecture on how a woman should be treated if a man was going to keep her in her place."

"Let me guess," she said with a wry twist of her lips. "Barefoot and pregnant were the preferred methods."

"Something like that. For the record, I don't agree with them."

"You must not have admitted that in front of them," she said as she let her gaze roam over his unmarked face. "They might have been inclined to rearrange a few of your features if they got the impression you disagreed with their Neanderthal point of view."

"I figured that out as I was tangled up with them on the floor." His gaze concentrated completely on her face. "I also had an interesting conversation with your friend, Harry the bartender. He cleared up a couple of misconceptions I had about your mother's health. You could have told me about her drinking problem, you know. Why didn't you?"

She shrugged, but the casual gesture was belied by the tension around her mouth and in her eyes. "My mother's devotion to alcohol isn't my favorite subject. Besides, you came to Nags Head to talk about your partner, not my mother."

"She is part of the package. You might have known your father all these years if she hadn't lied to you about his being dead."

After a moment's pause, Michele asked, "Tell me about him."

Cord had been in the process of taking a sip of coffee and nearly choked at her unexpected question. He coughed a couple of times, then, when he could breathe again, he asked, "What do you want to know?"

She shrugged. "I'm not sure. He's a complete stranger, yet we have a few genes and chromosomes in common. I suppose I'm curious. Considering he's still alive, I believe I can discount my mother's tale of my father being a weapons expert for the government, teaching our brave young men at Langley Air Force

Base, saving countless lives with his heroic deeds until a gun misfired and killed him.''

Her voice was calm, her hand steady when she raised the cup to her lips, yet Cord had a feeling she was stretched to the limit. Considering the type of day she'd had, he could understand if she was a little wired. She'd put in eight hours at the clinic and had hopped from one bar to another before nearly ending up in a barroom fight. On top of discovering the existence of a father who had voluntarily stayed out of her life for twenty-six years, Michele had been through a rough couple of days.

With that thought in mind, he suggested, ''Why don't we go into this another time, Michele? It's late, and we still have to find your mother.''

She shook her head. ''I'm not going to continue looking for her. It was dumb to even try, and I hate being stupid.'' She returned to the original subject. ''Tell me something about Michael Sutherland. Right now, he's only a name. I'd like to know about the person behind the name. How did you become business partners?''

Deciding she was the judge of what she could take, he asked, ''Do you want the short or the long version?''

''Whichever one is the truth. I'm not into fairy tales anymore.''

''Does that mean you once believed in fairy tales?'' he asked, even though he couldn't have said why it mattered.

''I once sucked my thumb, but I outgrew that, too.''

''There's nothing wrong with believing in a fairy tale or two.''

She stared at him. ''You believe in fairy tales?''

He shrugged. "Fairy tales, myths, fables, whatever term you want to use. Yeah, I guess I do. Some of them anyway. Being around salt-soaked boat captains and crews has given me a broad education, from the most boastful fish stories to some of the sights men have seen out at sea that defy explanation. Told over and over, these stories have become legends. I'd like to think there really are mermaids, a place called Atlantis and some descendants of Moby Dick still in the depths of the ocean."

His reply surprised her, especially since he was neither cynical, mocking or self-conscious when he gave her his answer. He had simply told her how he felt, without any apology or excuses as some men would.

Her own cynicism was deeply entrenched. "Maybe your belief in fairy tales is behind your stubborn push to reunite your partner with his daughter. You like happy endings."

With a shock, Cord realized she was right. He did like happy endings. He didn't necessarily expect one for himself, but he liked thinking such a thing was possible.

"Don't you believe in happy-ever-afters?"

"I'm not sure I even know what being happy is," she admitted, then scowled.

With surprising insight, he murmured, "You didn't mean to say that aloud, did you?"

"You were going to tell me how you and Michael Sutherland became partners."

He leaned back. "I've been around boats since I was twelve, and over the years, I've learned pretty much everything there is about the sea and about boats from bow to stern. I had had my captain's license for about a year when Michael approached me about going into business together. I'd met him a couple of times when he'd gone on a few fishing charters I took out on a boat belonging to a friend of mine. I knew Michael was a good sport about sharing the fish catches and didn't complain if he didn't hook on to a citation marlin every time he went out. Other than that, I didn't know much about him."

"Obviously you took him up on his offer."

"Not right away. One of Rocky's favorite sayings was 'If something sounds too good to be true, it usually is.'" He smiled faintly. "Another thing he used to say was that a boat skipper had salt water in his veins, a sponge for brains and the rest was pure jackass."

Michele was fascinated by the glimpse of affection she'd seen in his eyes. She wondered why it was so important to her to know he possessed that particular emotion.

"Who's Rocky?"

"A tough old sailor with a face like leather, hands like gnarled tree roots and a rough tongue that would make a sailor blush—and did, more than once. He taught me everything about the sea and boats." He looked down at the cup in his hand. "And just about everything else, I guess. He's the only one who thought I hadn't lost my mind when I went into business with Michael." After pausing for a few seconds, he tacked on, "I live on Rocky's boat. He left it to me when he died eight years ago."

Michele was curious about Cord's relationship with the old seaman but asked instead, "Why did everyone else think you were crazy to consider the offer from Michael Sutherland? Didn't he have a good business reputation?"

"It wasn't that." Cord finished his coffee, grimacing at the bite of bitterness from the bottom of the cup. "He was very successful in business. It's just that his expertise was in running a restaurant and a gift shop. He didn't know diddly about boats, fishing or booking charters. Suddenly, he was gung-ho about owning a fleet of boats without knowing the first thing about how to run them and make money."

"That's where you came in."

He shrugged. "I had the expertise but not much money to invest, so I thought he had one or two screws loose when he was so adamant about wanting me as a full partner. I couldn't bring anything to the corporation except experience and a captain's license. Michael insisted that was what he needed." Cord paused a few seconds, then went on, his voice oddly hesitant. "Lack of money has never been one of Michael's problems. His family has been rolling in it for several generations and quite a bit has tumbled his way."

Michele became annoyed when she heard the obvious reluctance in his voice as he mentioned his partner's financial situation. "You hated telling me that, didn't you? What's the matter, Cord? Are you afraid I'll want a share of the profits now that I know my old man has money?" She slid across the seat and put her hand on the table for balance as she got to her feet. "Money is the last thing I want or need from him, you or anyone else. Do me a favor. Take a long walk off a short pier and take your opinions with you."

Cord's fingers gripped her wrist to stop her from leaving. Several people glanced in their direction when she struggled to pull away from him, but he wasn't aware of anyone but Michele.

"I'm getting tired of you walking out on me, lady," he said in a taut voice. "Skip the snappy exit line for once." When she continued to resist, he added, "I'm bigger, stronger and more determined than you are, Michele. You aren't going anywhere without me until we work this out."

Michele didn't sit down, but she stopped trying to get away from him. "Which means until I agree to come to Virginia Beach."

"The man is dying, Michele," he said with feeling. "Your father is dying. Would it be so much to ask of you to see him so he can make peace with himself and with you before he runs out of time?"

The long day, the worry associated with her mother and the unfair demands Cord was putting on her suddenly became too much. Her voice was deadly calm. "There were times when I was a child that I had to make decisions no child should be expected to make, because I had no one to turn to for advice. Instead of playing with other kids after school, I was trying to figure out how to pay the rent and buy food because my mother had spent her paycheck on a drinking binge. While other girls were having sleepovers, I was trying to get Faith from her car into our house in the middle of the night before she passed out."

Cord could almost feel the pain evident in her voice and in her eyes. "Michele, you don't have to do this."

She wasn't finished. "Before I went to school, I went around the cottage and picked up empty vodka and gin bottles. When I came home from school, I never knew what I would find. Sometimes dinner would be burning in the oven and she would be passed out on the couch, or she would have invited a few of her drinking buddies over for a party. There were more times than I want to count when I did my homework between mixing drinks and cleaning up spilled whiskey or gin or vodka. Where was Michael Sutherland then, Cord? Out fishing on your boat? Eating at his restaurant? Counting the daily receipts from the sale of souvenirs to the tourists? Starting yet another business?" She took a deep, ragged breath. "Trying to claim any type of relationship after all this time would be a farce on both sides. If you can't see that, you're blind."

Cord stood and leaned toward her until his head was only inches away from hers. "At least you have a chance to ask him what the hell he thought he was doing by ignoring you all that time," he said in a deadly soft voice.

"You don't understand," she murmured, suddenly exhausted.

Cord said a soft curse under his breath. Then he tightened his grip on her wrist and drew her away from the table toward the door. Once outside, his long fast strides made it necessary for Michele to practically run in order to keep up with him. Since he had an unyielding grip on her arm, she had no choice but to keep up with him.

He stopped abruptly near her car and pressed her against the door. He placed his hands on the roof on either side of her, effectively caging her between him and the car.

"I understand more than you think," he said harshly. "My mother left me at a shopping mall when I was twelve years old."

He ignored her shocked gasp and went on. "She bought me an ice cream cone—a double-dip chocolate chip, which was my favorite—and told me to sit on one of the benches and eat it while she shopped. She said she might be gone for quite some time, but I was to stay there until she got back. Hours later, the security guard rousted me out because the mall was closing. I slept outside the entrance under some bushes that night and went back to the same bench the next day. It finally occurred to me she wasn't coming back when the mall was about to close the second night. I left before the guard could run me off. I never saw her again."

Stunned, she asked quietly, "What did you do?"

"The same thing you did. I played the cards I'd been dealt. But there's one difference between our childhoods, Michele. A big difference. You have the opportunity to get some answers about the past." He stepped back. "You'd be a damn fool to pass up this chance to confront your father and demand that he explain why he abandoned you. It's a hell of a lot more than I'll ever have."

Michele murmured, "I'm sorry."

"I don't want your sympathy. I want a lot of things from you, but sympathy isn't one of them."

He slid his hand around the back of her neck. His fingers caressed the taut cords in her neck while his thumb stroked her throat. He watched her steadily.

"Cord?"

"This doesn't have anything to do with Michael and is probably a damn good reason for you to stay the hell away from Virginia Beach." His thumb moved over her jawline. "I want you."

Shock rolled through her at his blunt honesty. "You don't even know me."

He smiled crookedly. "I think that's part of the problem. I knew more about you than you did when we met. I knew you had a father who is very much alive. From what your old school chum told me, you have always been a private person, keeping people at a distance on purpose."

"What old school chum?"

"Harry, the bartender. If he didn't work in a bar, he wouldn't have known about your mother, either. From what he said, not many people know about your mother's fondness for booze. I know about her, your father and your fetish for gaudy socks. People who've known you for years don't know that much about you." His gaze went to her mouth. "I'm also a threat to you because you're attracted to me as much as I am to you."

She didn't deny it. Michele's breath caught in her throat when he leaned closer. "Cord, this is crazy."

"I know. You make me crazy. I need to see if I can make you a little crazy, too. I'd hate to think I'm the only one suffering."

The last thought she had was that she should stop him. Then his mouth covered hers, and she could no longer think at all. Anger and frustrated desire made a heady mixture when he claimed the moist intimacy of her mouth.

Cord's hunger wasn't satisfied but grew more ravenous when he felt her respond. Her body went slack against him, and she raised her hands to his waist, whether to hold him closer or to push him away, he had no way of knowing. He could easily saturate himself with the taste of her, except it wouldn't be enough.

Michele felt as though the earth had suddenly tilted under her feet. The power of his male hunger was both exhilarating and frightening. She was being swept away by a fierce need as he slanted his mouth over hers to deepen the kiss.

A few breathless moments later, Cord broke off the assault on her mouth and buried his face in the curve of her throat and shoulder. He held her tightly, taking deep breaths as he fought to regain his control.

The kiss was supposed to have been a test to see how she would react. It wasn't supposed to make him feel desperate for more.

Because of his own reaction, more than hers, he felt the need to set the boundaries of his involvement.

"I don't have a lot of faith in people's staying power, even my own. It's only fair that I warn you not to expect a lifetime commitment from me. I'll take care of you when we become lovers, but I won't be responsible for another person's happiness ever again, not even temporarily. You'll be with me because you want me, and for no other reason. We can enjoy each other as long as it lasts. Think about that while you're mulling over whether you should come to Virginia Beach or not."

Cord didn't give her a chance to argue, comment or even take a much-needed breath. She stared after him as he walked away from her.

Michele sank back against the car, feeling as though she'd been blown apart by hurricane-force winds.

Chapter Eight

Michele read the sign at the side of the road that welcomed her and everyone else to Virginia Beach, Virginia. Her faint smile had a cynical edge to it as she drove by. At least the city council of the seaside town was putting out the welcome mat. She wasn't that sure of her reception with Michael Sutherland. Cord had insisted that he wanted to see her, and had made several attempts to convince her of that. Soon, she would know whether he'd been telling the truth or not.

She wished she could be sure she was doing the right thing, not only for herself but for Michael Sutherland, too. He might be expecting more from her than she would be able to give, especially if he wanted her to pretend the past twenty-six years hadn't happened. Once she had learned of his existence, Michele couldn't get past the fact that he had known he had a daughter and hadn't tried to contact her before. At least not that she knew about. One consistent argument had persuaded her that she needed to talk to Michael Sutherland: If her mother had lied about his death, she could also have concealed any attempt he might have made to see Michele. Michele needed to know the truth.

If he was expecting some grand reunion, however, he was going to be disappointed. She couldn't pretend instant affection for someone she didn't know. Her experience with a father figure was nonexistent, unless she counted Doc Mooney, the vet she used to trail after like a small shadow. He'd been remarkably patient, answering the barrage of questions about animals she'd fired at him, but he'd always maintained a distance she had sensed and respected. He had been kind, but she had never thought of him as a substitute father.

Cord had been right when he said she had to see her father or she would always wonder what Michael Sutherland was like. If she didn't confront him, she would also speculate about the reasons why he had walked out of her life when she was a child.

She had found it easier than she expected to make the arrangements to have a day free. When she'd asked Bud to take her appointments on Saturday, she had almost wished he'd say no, making it impossible for her to take the trip to Virginia Beach. He hadn't objected. Saturdays were their busiest day of the week, but he'd pointed out that she'd been generous about the time he'd taken for his honeymoon. He owed her one.

If he made her look at all his honeymoon photographs, he was going to owe her more than that, she thought with tolerant amusement, but she kept that to herself.

Taking a day off was enough of an unusual occurrence to cause comment from Bud. Combined with Cord's visit to the lunchroom that he knew about, it was inevitable that Bud would make an opportunity to gently but persistently drill her about her plans.

"Is your car still acting up?" he asked casually while Michele peered into the small eye of a microscope in the lab.

"I took it in for a tune-up. Why?"

As she replaced one slide with another, he answered, "I was just thinking how inconvenient it would be for you to have car trouble during your trip to Virginia Beach."

"I thought of that, which is why I took it into Earl's yesterday." She raised her head and saw his grin. "Very clever. How did you know I was going to Virginia Beach?"

"Elementary, my dear Michele." He counted off his brilliant deductions on his fingers. "Cord Thomas is from Virginia Beach. He had a predatory gleam in his eye the other day in the lunchroom. You've never taken any time off from work since I've known you, and lately I've seen you stare off into space at odd moments. Speaking as one who has recently been bitten by the love bug, I can recognize another victim."

"I'm impressed with your reasoning ability, but I have other reasons for going to Virginia Beach. And you still don't get your raise until June."

"Ah, shucks." He half sat on the edge of the table. "So, do Rita and I need to start saving up for a wedding gift, or what?"

Michele gave up trying to concentrate on the diagnostic slides. Leaning back in her chair, she said, "I haven't even been out with the man—unless you count a cup of coffee at a fast-food restaurant, which I paid for—and you already have us walking down the aisle. I do plan on seeing him when I'm in Virginia Beach, but it will be in connection with other business I need to take care of while I'm there. You're making something out of nothing."

"Yeah, right," he said smugly. "And he doesn't look at you as though you're lunch, and he's hungry. If you didn't notice, you need glasses."

She'd noticed. That was only one of the problems she had to face in Virginia Beach. An even bigger complication was her reaction to Cord. She preferred being in control, knowing what lay ahead before she walked into an unfamiliar area. From her earliest memory, she had proceeded cautiously, never leaping into a situation unprepared if she could help it.

In the short time she'd known Cord, she'd stumbled over emotions and desires that threatened to trip her up.

And Cord wasn't the only reason she had for being apprehensive about her trip out of town. This was not the best time to leave Nags Head with her mother acting as though Prohibition were right around the corner, but Edith Walcott had been frank when she reminded Michele that Faith would find a way to get a drink whether either of them were there or not. Unfortunately that was true.

Faith's latest night out had ended quietly with a ride back to the cottage from a cocktail waitress. She'd been considerate of Mrs. Walcott by sleeping in Mrs. Walcott's car until morning rather than waking her.

Or perhaps she just hadn't been able to make it up the stairs.

Mrs. Walcott promised to be extra vigilant while Michele was out of town, if that would ease the younger woman's mind. Michele didn't have the heart to tell Mrs. Walcott that she couldn't remember a single day when she hadn't worried about her mother. Distance wouldn't change that.

Michele took the precaution of keeping the reason for her trip from Faith. Mentioning Michael Sutherland's name the other night had been the catalyst for her latest binge, and Michele didn't want to give her an excuse for another one. Lord knows what her mother would do if she found out that Michele was going to see her father, who was very much alive.

There would never be a good time in her mother's mind for her to meet the man Faith had pronounced dead. Michele knew that, but putting off the trip wouldn't make the initial meeting any easier. Remembering what Cord had said about his partner's health, she knew that delaying the trip even a few days might prevent the possibility of her confronting her father at all.

Michele had to prepare herself to see Cord again. It was impossible to forget how thoroughly he had proved that the attraction between them existed. The devastating kiss they'd shared had shaken her to the bone. Considering the distance between Nags Head and Virginia Beach, having any sort of relationship would be nearly impossible, although he'd implied it was inevitable. Still, Michele couldn't deny she had responded to him with a great deal of enthusiasm and not a little amount of passion.

She had no idea how she would react when she saw him again. During the few days following their last explosive meeting, Michele hadn't needed to do or say anything at all to Cord. He hadn't called or showed up at the clinic or at her home. He'd simply walked away that night after kissing her senseless. Then he had checked out of his hotel and returned to Virginia Beach.

The next move was up to her. What had her rolling and tossing at night was the question of whether or not she should take that last big step.

For several days, she had thought of little else but Michael Sutherland and Cord Thomas. Both men represented possible rejection and probable pain in different ways, but she didn't see how she could ignore either man now.

She had to finish what Cord had started.

When doing surgery on an animal, she didn't stop halfway through the procedure. She used her knowledge and skill to bring the operation to a satisfactory conclusion. Once she completed this episode in her life, perhaps she could begin to make peace with her past.

Early Saturday morning, she left Nags Head. She inserted an audiotape of a recent bestseller in the car's cassette player to give herself something else to concentrate on besides thinking about what was waiting ahead. Two hours later, she ejected the last tape and wondered what the story had been about. Her mind had flitted around like a demented butterfly, unable to settle on any one thing.

Stopping at a traffic light, she glanced down at the slip of paper that contained the directions to Sutherland Landing. She hadn't needed to resort to a private investigator to find the address as Michael Sutherland had to locate her. All it had required was a few minutes with the telephone directory for the Tidewater area of Virginia. A few phone calls later and a few minutes studying a street map, and she'd been prepared to take the trip to the popular resort town.

After only one wrong turn, Michele found the marina. Sea gulls soared overhead as she got out of her station wagon. The parking area was adjacent to a large beachfront restaurant with a number of floating boat slips extending out from several wide aluminum docks that rose and fell with the tides.

Michele gazed over the boats in the water. If there were any under thirty feet, she couldn't see them. The majority were forty- to fifty-foot-long fishing vessels with towering flying bridges and extended outriggers for catching large citation fish.

She looked around for a sign or an arrow, something to indicate where the Sutherland Marina office was located. If Cord wasn't there, she hoped someone in the office could tell her where she could find him. She started walking down the ramp leading to the boat slips.

A man with a gray-stubbled jaw, dressed in jeans that were dangerously thin and almost white with age and numerous washings, was sitting on an upturned five-gallon bucket, smoking a pipe as he leaned against a dock piling. He reminded Michele of a bored tomcat who would simply ignore anyone who dared to bother him.

"Excuse me," she said politely. "Could you tell me where I could find Cord Thomas?"

His attention went to the stem of the pipe in his hand. "I could," he replied in a voice rough as gravel. "Question is, why should I?"

Michele heard a tinge of a New England accent. Amused rather than annoyed, she asked, "I can't think of a single reason why you shouldn't. You'll have to take my word that I'm not selling anything or collecting bills."

"Last time I directed a pretty young thing to his boat, Cord about stripped two layers of skin off me. Told me if he wanted a woman on his boat, he'd get one."

Michele hoped Cord didn't have a pretty young thing on board at the moment. "What if I was a potential client who wanted to charter a boat?"

The man raised his head and took his time examining her taupe leather shoes, pleated slacks and white vest with taupe-embroidered designs worn under a silk suit jacket.

"I don't think so," he murmured. "You don't look much like the fishing type."

Michele wasn't about to ask him what type of woman he thought she looked like. He just might tell her, and she needed all the confidence she could muster right now.

"If you mean the type that catches fish, you're right, I'm not," she said agreeably. "I haven't had the time to go fishing in years. I have treated a couple of exotic fish and a sand shark recently, but I guess that doesn't count."

A male voice behind her said, "It counts."

She turned. Cord was standing so close, she would only have to raise her arm and she would be touching him. It was tempting.

The sun was shining directly into his eyes, which she hoped accounted for the way he was frowning and squinting. A streak of oil was spread diagonally across the front of his white T-shirt as though he'd swiped his hand over it. The jeans he wore hadn't been around as long as the other man's, but the splotches of oil on his thighs and hips matched the ones on his shirt.

He looked wonderful, she thought. When all he did was stare at her without speaking, she said ruefully, "I evidently should have called first."

Instead of answering, Cord took her hand as he stepped over a water hose stretched across the dock and brushed past her. She was neatly turned and drawn along with him.

The other man chuckled and drawled, "I guess you aren't going to throw this one back, huh, Cord?"

Over his shoulder, Cord replied, "Nope. This one's a keeper, Orren."

Even though he seemed to be in a hurry, he slowed his pace to accommodate her shorter stride. Michele made a wild guess and assumed he was taking her to his boat since they were walking away from the shore.

Cord didn't release her hand when he stepped aboard a boat named *Rocky Road*. She used the step he had ignored and joined him on the aft deck.

"You don't seemed surprised to see me," she commented.

He wasn't through dragging her around with him, it seemed. Sliding open a door, he drew her into the curtained interior.

Closing the door, he laced his fingers through hers. "Surprise doesn't quite cover it. Shock comes closer." Glancing at their joined hands, he murmured, "Sorry.

I've been working on an engine. You'll have to wash your hands.''

She smiled. "I've had messier things on my hands than oil and grease. Don't worry about it."

"I'm glad you changed your mind about seeing Michael." His fingers slid restlessly over hers, clenching and unclenching, stroking and clasping. "And it isn't only because of Michael. It's good to see you again."

"I'm still not sure I'm doing the right thing by coming here," she admitted. "Part of me wants everything to stay the way it was."

His fingers tightened around hers as he pointed out, "That's not possible. Not now."

Michele suddenly found it difficult to breathe when his gaze lowered to her mouth.

"Damn," he muttered under his breath. "I can't even kiss you. I'm filthy."

"We're surrounded by water," she reminded him. "Add some soap and some clean clothes, and you'll be ready."

A corner of his lips curved upward. "The soap and water I'll go along with. As for clothing..." He let whatever he'd been about to say drift off. "I've thought a lot about you since the night we toured the bars of Nags Head. In fact, I've been finding it difficult to think of anything else, although to be honest, my thoughts have gone beyond kissing."

Her heartbeat thudded heavily like a dropped shoe. There was a teasing glint in his eyes, but she sensed he was also serious.

"Let's take one thing at a time, starting with Michael Sutherland. You might want to find that soap and water first, but that's up to you."

He blinked. "What are you talking about?"

"I'm going to visit Michael Sutherland before I lose my nerve or change my mind again, whichever comes first. Since you're responsible for my being here, you should go with me." She couldn't read his expression, and since he didn't say anything, she had no way of knowing what he was thinking. "Unless this is a bad time," she added hesitantly. "Has his health gotten worse?"

Cord slowly shook his head. "He's about the same."

She didn't have the patience to play guessing games. "Then what is it? You've been nagging me to come to Virginia Beach to see your partner. I'm here, so what's the problem?"

He smiled suddenly. "There's no problem. I didn't expect to be so happy to see you, that's all," he said frankly. "And it has nothing to do with Michael." Leaning down, he touched his mouth lightly to hers. "I'll get cleaned up. There are some cold drinks in the fridge in the galley. Help yourself."

Releasing her hand after pressing her fingers briefly, Cord walked across the gray carpet to several descending steps. A few seconds later, he disappeared behind a teak louvered door.

Michele was still standing where he'd left her when she heard the sound of a shower running. She hadn't realized how tense she was until she took a deep breath and felt some of the tension seep away.

When she accepted his offer of a cold drink by opening the refrigerator, the contents inside weren't what she expected. Instead of six-packs of beer and smelly containers of bait, she found bottled water, juice, soft drinks, at least four kinds of cheese, fruit and a variety of sliced meats. Several containers of yogurt were also a surprise.

Perhaps she should stop making assumptions and accept Cord for who he was and not who she expected him to be.

Taking a can of cola from his refrigerator, Michele glanced around the small galley. The electric stove, aluminum sink, teak cabinets and microwave were spotlessly clean. The counter was bare, all utensils put away in their proper place.

Returning to the salon, Michele took in the matching teal-colored settees, the wet bar, entertainment center and drop-leaf table. Like the galley, the salon was spotless and tidy. She walked over to the entertainment center and read through some of the titles on the extensive supply of CDs and cassettes. Cord's music preferences ran the gamut from country to classics, with some light rock and some jazz filling in the gaps.

Below a small-screen television set were two rows of hardcover and paperback books. Scanning their titles, she found Cord's reading tastes were as varied as his music. A neighboring stack of videos revealed a number of documentaries on foreign countries, which outnumbered popular movies.

Michele became curious about a series of videos that had handwritten labels stuck on the sides of the cases. One in particular, with Rocky-Test printed in bold black letters, caught her attention. She turned on the television set and slid the videotape cassette into the VCR after turning it on. She pushed the play button and stepped back so she could see the screen.

The images flickered, then settled, showing a short, stocky man at the helm on the flying bridge of a boat.

His face was only partially visible below a baseball cap and above a bushy gray beard. He was wearing yellow rain gear with the collar up around his neck, and a cigar appeared to be permanently embedded in the corner of his mouth. The stogie certainly didn't inhibit his speech and bobbed up and down like an orchestra conductor's baton whenever he spoke. Which was often.

She grinned broadly after watching the screen for several minutes.

Michele had never heard the English language accentuated with such a colorful array of cuss words. Oddly enough, his language wasn't disgusting profanity but mostly an imaginative use of descriptive terms for material found on the bottom of farmers' boots.

As Michele watched the screen, she was so intent on the images in front of her, she wasn't aware that the shower was no longer running.

The camera lens panned to the person standing next to Rocky, who was also wearing rain gear but no hat, his dark hair wet from the spray caused by the bow of the boat cutting through the rough sea. Cord was younger, in his midtwenties perhaps, his face thinner and less mature than it was now.

After watching for several minutes, Michele realized the film was supposed to be a promotional video to advertise fishing charters. She had been momentarily fascinated by the older man's picturesque speech and hadn't paid much attention to the rest of what he was saying. She gathered this particular part of the video was a description of the various high-tech equipment available on board. The unlit cigar bounced up and down as Rocky pointed out the blankety-blank depth finder and the expletive radar.

Michele chuckled as Rocky described the piece of equipment used as an aid to find fish underwater. Every third or fourth word didn't have a thing to do with fish, but certainly added variety to an otherwise dry, technical explanation.

Cord's voice was amused as he joined her to watch the video. "Rocky's original plan was to buy a minute or two of air time at a local television station to advertise Rocky Road Charters. The one you're watching is a test copy taken by the video company."

Turning her head, she saw he was only a foot away from her. His soiled shirt and jeans had been replaced by a wine-colored cotton shirt and a pair of black jeans. Cord's black hair was damp from his recent shower and an attempt had been made to discipline the thick strands with a comb.

Amused by the video, Michele asked, "Did he pass the test?"

"What do you think?"

"The commercial would never be shown during Saturday-morning cartoons."

"Or any other time," he agreed with a grin. "We eventually went with the shot on the bridge of the equipment—without Rocky's commentary. I recorded a separate audio that went with it."

Michele turned her attention back to the video. Rocky had turned the helm over to Cord and was making his way down the ladder. She caught only a brief glimpse of the younger Cord, who was standing with his legs slightly apart for balance and with one hand on the helm.

After he disappeared from view, she asked, "How old were you when this video was made?"

"I don't know. Maybe twenty-five, twenty-six. It was a year or two after my divorce."

Jerking her head around, she stared at him, shock widening her eyes. "How long were you married?"

"A couple of very long years. For both of us. It was a mistake from the beginning. Rocky tried to tell me so at the time, but of course, I wouldn't listen."

"Is your divorce the reason you said you weren't going to be responsible for anyone ever again?"

He looked at her with a puzzled expression in his eyes. "When did I say that?"

"The night I went looking for my mother. When you warned me not to expect anything from you but an affair."

Frowning, he murmured, "I don't remember saying that."

"Those might not have been your exact words, but it's my interpretation of what you meant. Was I wrong?"

Cord didn't want to take the chance of misunderstanding her. "And you came anyway. Does that mean you're ready to accept my terms?"

"It means I'm agreeing to see Michael Sutherland," she replied, stalling, aware she hadn't completely answered his question. "Isn't that what you wanted?"

"Among other things," he drawled. "That was the general plan in the beginning. It's amazing the changes that can happen to a man's priorities in such a short time. I still want you to see Michael for his sake, as well as your own, but I admit I'm pleased you came to me first."

Michele found the warmth in his eyes disturbing on a deeper level than she understood.

"Sometimes our choices are made for us," she said.

"Meaning?"

She smiled. "I don't know where Michael Sutherland lives."

Cord heeded one of Rocky's bits of wisdom by not reeling in the line too fast and facing the possibility of losing the catch. The more time he spent with Michele, the more fascinated he became by his reaction to her.

"I'll take you to him." His gray eyes held hers like a powerful magnet. "I used the phone in the master stateroom to call him to prepare him for your visit."

Now that she was so close to meeting her father, she hesitated. "Are you sure he's up to seeing me?"

"I checked with his doctor before I went to Nags Head to find you, just in case meeting you might cause too much excitement for him. Apparently there is good stress and bad stress. He's supposed to stay away from business problems for a while. Being reunited with his daughter is classified as good stress."

He took the can of cola out of her hand and brought it to his lips. His gaze remained on her mouth as he drank.

The simple act of sharing a drink seemed oddly intimate; Michele's blood suddenly pumped heavily in her veins, as though she'd been running up a steep hill. She didn't find it as easy to operate on two levels as he did, talking about one reason for her visit and physically communicating the other to her. Who was she trying to kid? she wondered. He didn't have to do anything to strengthen the attraction simmering between them. Her feelings were growing rapidly, almost too fast for her mind to keep up.

"I'm curious." He handed the can back to her. "What made you change your mind about seeing your father?"

"It was something you said."

"I said a lot of things," he stated with a small smile, drawing her gaze briefly to his mouth. "I wasn't sure you heard a single word."

"I heard you. As you've probably already guessed, I'm not an impulsive person. Someone had to be practical and sensible while I was growing up. I was elected. It's become second nature. I needed a little time to think about the consequences."

His eyes narrowed, his sharp gaze intent on her face. "Of seeing me or Michael?"

"Both," she said frankly.

"Well, that's honest enough. What kind of consequences did you come up with?"

Michele walked over to one of the stools positioned in front of the drop-leaf table and sat down. Setting the cola can on the polished surface, she said, "The only close involvement I've ever had with another person is with my mother, which doesn't give me much incentive to willingly walk into another one. I've basically been a caretaker, always providing my mother with what she needed. With Faith, I always knew what she wanted. I don't know what Michael wants from me. Or what you want."

"The day I met you in your office, you expected me to want something from you."

"At least I'm consistent."

Cord closed the distance between them and sat down on the other stool. He needed to touch her, and she needed to be touched. Taking her hands in his, he said quietly, "I don't just want *something*. I want you. Is that so hard for you to accept?"

Her gaze had lowered to their joined hands. Then she looked up. "Yes, it is."

Cord saw the wariness in her eyes and the tension around her mouth. He wasn't prepared for the rush of protectiveness blending with the desire hardening his body. Her vulnerability brought out a streak of possessiveness he didn't know he had, but that didn't stop him from recognizing the emotion.

So much for staying uninvolved, he thought.

"Life really throws us some funny curves sometimes, doesn't it? I swore I'd never get involved with another woman after my divorce, and you didn't plan on taking on another emotional commitment on top of your mother. Whether either one of us likes it or not, Michele, we can't deny there's something between us."

"That's what scares me," she admitted honestly.

"Me, too." He smiled when she raised a skeptical brow. "Women don't have a monopoly on insecurity. There's an unwritten law in the macho code that prevents men from confessing we don't always know what we're doing when it comes to dealing with the female of the species."

Her mouth curved into a smile. "Do we flip a coin to decide if we stop now or go on?"

He shook his head slowly as he rose to his feet and drew her up with him. "We can be more creative than that."

He lifted a hand to the side of her face, his other hand resting on her shoulder. His gaze locked with hers as he applied pressure to bring her closer.

Her body shivered in reaction when she felt his hard body against hers. Because she was unable to deny her own desire, she obeyed the demand his nearness made within her.

Cord slowly threaded his fingers through her hair, holding her still as he lowered his head, giving her time to stop him if that was what she wanted. Michele could have ceased breathing easier than she could resist the desire surging through her.

She was drawn down into a whirlpool of passion, which threatened to drown her when he deepened the assault on her mouth. Michele sank into the passionate waves of sensations dragging her down into a vortex of aching need.

Hearing his hoarse groan when he broke away to bury his lips in the curve of her neck, she realized with amazement that he was as caught up in the tumultuous urgency of desire as she was.

His hands were on her back and her hips, holding her tightly, possessively, against the contours of his body until she was molded to him. He trembled against her when she raked her fingers through the dark damp strands of his hair.

"Michele," he groaned, just before claiming her mouth with devastating male hunger that nearly swamped her completely.

Suddenly his hands clutched at her hips. He lifted his head so he could look into her eyes. His voice rasped like torn raw silk. "We're in deeper than I thought."

Michele laid her forehead against his shoulder in defeat, unable to fight the taunting attraction between them any longer.

"I don't understand this," she whispered, more to herself than to him. "We hardly know each other and yet..."

"And yet we nearly go up in flames when we touch each other," he finished for her. While he still could, he released her. "I could say I'll give you time, Michele, but I don't have much resistance with you, especially when you respond to me the way you just did. After we see Michael, I'd like to come back here. It will be up to you whether you return to Nags Head today or tomorrow morning."

She raised her hand to her forehead. "Oh, Lord. I forgot about Michael."

His smile contained male satisfaction along with humor. "Don't feel bad. For a few minutes there, I forgot my own name." He held out his hand. "Come on. Let's get this over with. If we don't leave now, I'll kiss you again, and Michael will have a long wait."

Cord offered to drive, but Michele insisted on taking her car. It gave her a sense of being in control of the situation if she was responsible for getting herself there. The excuse sounded feeble even to her, and she certainly wasn't about to tell it to him. She needed all the confidence she could find, whatever way she could find it.

Following Cord's directions, Michele drove slowly along the winding, narrow, tree-lined road leading into a neighborhood of expensive, sprawling houses. The owners were apparently the kind of people who could afford to buy three lots to build on one and leave the others on either side vacant to give them the extra acreage they desired. Michele knew from studying the city map that most of the houses in this section were positioned near the Lynnhaven River, constructed so that only the owner would benefit from the view. Acres of land, thick foliage, abundant trees and, occasionally, high privacy fences prevented anyone driving by from getting a glimpse of the river and, in some cases, the houses themselves.

Michele was glad Cord knew the way and she didn't have to look for Michael Sutherland's property on her own. Searching for house numbers would be nearly impossible. Michele had to look hard in order to even find mailboxes. One number was partially covered with vines, another was painted on a large gray landscape rock in elaborate if barely readable script. Addresses were tacked on a tree, a fence post; some were so discreetly marked, the house numbers couldn't be seen at all.

When Cord pointed out a driveway ahead, Michele spotted four brass numbers tacked vertically on a rustic post to the right of a driveway lined with plump azalea bushes and tall fir trees. Because she was driving slowly, she was able to see the mailbox painted dark green to match the foliage of the bushes. The name Sutherland was spelled out in brass letters on a flat strip of painted wood attached to the curved top.

Michele's nervousness increased now that she was so close to meeting the man who, although a complete stranger, was her father. She had faced a rabid pit bull and, with less trepidation, had taken thorns out of a cranky raccoon. She could tell herself she was being silly, but that didn't stop her stomach from reacting as though she were on a runaway roller coaster.

With her pulse beating loudly in her ears, Michele followed the curving driveway leading up to a large white brick house. Parking in front, Michele studied the home belonging to her father. The middle section was three stories high, the rooms located on either side on ground level. The double-door entrance and the shutters were made of stained dark wood. The windows sparkled in spots of sunlight that somehow managed to get through the foliage that grew profusely on the property.

Michele's first reaction was that the house was exceptionally large for one man to live in. Evidently Cord hadn't been exaggerating when he'd said Michael Sutherland was comfortable financially.

After she turned off the engine, Michele heard the sound of squeaking brakes and the rumbling engine of a large vehicle. Glancing in the rearview mirror, she caught a glimpse of a white van with lettering on the side pulling away from the driveway. Michele watched the vehicle until it disappeared behind some trees.

While she still had her nerve, she reached for her purse. She wasn't aware her hand was trembling until Cord's fingers covered hers.

"He's just as nervous to meet you as you are to meet him."

"I'm not sure that's possible," she said with a ghost of a laugh. "It's silly, I know, but I can't seem to help it. Butterflies are turning cartwheels in my stomach."

His fingers tightened over hers briefly. "It's understandable." He released her hand and opened the passenger door. "He's probably pacing the floor. Come on. Once you meet him, you'll find you've worried about nothing."

Michele took a deep, steadying breath before opening her door. She wondered if this was how a condemned man felt taking that long walk to the gallows. She knew she had to make the trip, but she wasn't looking forward to reaching her final destination.

Just after she closed the car door, Michele heard a young voice in the distance calling, "Uncle Cord!"

Michele looked down the driveway and saw a girl, who was perhaps thirteen or fourteen, running toward them, her face lit up like a Christmas tree at the sight of Cord. She was carrying a small oblong black case by its handle.

The young girl threw herself at Cord when she was close enough, and he hugged her back. "I'm glad to see you too, Hannah-banana," he said with amusement as she nearly choked him with her slender arms around his neck.

Michele hadn't a clue who the teenager was, but she was amused by the hero worship in the girl's eyes.

Cord glanced at the case in her hand. "I forgot about your flute lesson today. Was that Terry's mother who dropped you off?"

"Yeah." The young girl grimaced. "She's one of the band mothers this year. She wants the boys in the band to wear black for the Thanksgiving concert and the girls to wear orange frilly dresses. We'll look like pumpkins."

"It could be worse. She could suggest the girls wear black and the boys wear orange."

Grinning up at him, Hannah asked, "Are you here to see Daddy again?"

"Yeah, and to see how you did on that history test yesterday."

"I aced it." With the bluntness of youth, she added, "You were here this morning, Uncle Cord. Usually you only come once a day." A serious look replaced the bright smile. "He's okay, isn't he? Daddy was all right when I left."

"He's fine."

That wasn't entirely true, as they both knew. The man had recently had a heart attack, which made his health vulnerable until he got his strength back, but Hannah needed reassuring, so Cord gave it to her.

He then happened to look across the top of the car and was startled by how pale Michele had suddenly become. The knuckles of the hand clasping the shoulder strap of her purse were white, her eyes dark with shock.

She was staring at Hannah, a stricken expression in her eyes.

Chapter Nine

Icy-cold needles pierced Cord's composure when it dawned on him what was wrong. Michele hadn't known about her father's other family.

From the few innocent comments Hannah made, Michele had come to the only conclusion possible: the young girl's father was Michael Sutherland, and she lived with him in his large home. Cord realized Michele would consider her father's neglect of her even worse, knowing he had stuck around for his other daughter but not for her.

Cursing himself for not telling her about Michael's second marriage, he tried to make up for it now. "Hannah, this is—"

Raising her hand in a gesture halting whatever he'd been about to say, Michele introduced herself to the young girl who was looking at her with friendly curiosity. "I'm Michele LaBrock, Hannah. I came along with Cord to meet your father and to wish him a speedy recovery. But if it's not convenient, I can come another time.''

Hannah walked around the car to where Michele stood. "He likes company. I'm sure he'd want to meet you. You're very pretty."

"Thank you." Somehow Michele managed a small smile. "So are you."

And she was, thought Michele. The girl's silky brown hair was pulled away from her delicate face by a large hair clip on the crown of her head, the rest of the long strands falling on her back below her delicate shoulders. She wore a pink cotton sweater and a pair of blue pleated slacks. She looked young and vital, her brown eyes sparkling with life and enthusiasm that made Michele suddenly feel old and jaded.

Thankfully, Michele couldn't find any resemblance to any of her own features, which might have caused the girl to ask questions Michele wasn't prepared to answer.

Cord approached Michele and saw her stiffen her spine when he came near her. The barriers were solidly in place again. Rage seared through him. Any trust she'd begun to have in him was lost now that she realized he'd kept a vital bit of information from her. Although he hadn't purposely neglected to tell her about Michael's second family, he didn't think that little detail was going to matter to Michele.

His excuse was that his extreme reaction to her and the unusual situation had muddled his thinking to the point where he actually forgot about mentioning that Michael had remarried and divorced a second wife.

And had custody of the two children from that marriage.

The shock of learning she had a half sister was going to be compounded once Michele found she had a half brother, as well. The hole Cord had inadvertently dug for himself was getting deeper.

Cursing himself for being so stupid and Michael for putting him in this position, he said quietly, "Michael is waiting for us."

Michele didn't move toward the house. "I'll stay here with Hannah while you see Michael and tell him who I am."

"Damn it, Michele," he said under his breath.

Meeting his gaze, she added, "And who I'm not. Do you understand?"

She wanted him to tell Michael that she didn't want him to acknowledge the blood tie between them in front of Hannah.

"Michele . . ."

"Or I go back to Nags Head now."

"That won't accomplish anything," he said quietly.

"Neither will creating problems where none exist now."

Hannah's presence prevented Cord from doing what he wanted. Which was to kick something or cuss a blue streak in frustration. Or attempt to shake some sense into Michele.

Or take her in his arms until the haunted look in her eyes went away. But he knew she wouldn't allow him to touch her. Not now, at least. He wouldn't accept never.

Because Hannah was there, it was damn difficult to speak frankly to Michele. She'd made it clear she didn't want Hannah to know of her relationship to Michael, and as much as Cord hated stretching the truth any further than it already was, he didn't see where he had a choice. Even shocked as she must be, Michele had the presence of mind to know it was up to her father to tell Hannah about his other daughter, he realized. Michele didn't want that time to be now.

"All right," he agreed. "We'll do it your way."

Hannah looked back and forth between Cord and Michele several times, clearly confused by the terse conversation between the adults. "Is something wrong?"

Michele answered before Cord could. "Nothing's wrong. If you have some time to spare, I'd like to see the river if you wouldn't mind showing it to me. On the way here, Cord told me about the remnants of an old fishing boat that sank just offshore and can be seen in the water. Would you mind showing it to me while Cord talks to your father?"

Hannah looked at Cord for direction. "I usually let Daddy know I'm home from practice, so he doesn't worry."

Cord studied Michele's expression for a full five seconds. All her well-honed defenses were firmly back in place, he noticed, and he wanted to tear them down with his bare hands.

He told Hannah, "Go along with Michele. I'll tell him you're with your—"

Michele's head snapped around, her eyes glaring at him.

"Your new friend," he finished lamely, replacing the word *sister*. "You can see your father in a few minutes."

"Okay." Hannah handed her flute case to Cord to take inside with him and smiled at Michele. "We'll go around the house this way. You might like to see the fountain where Neal fell in on his sixteenth birthday last year. It was so funny. Daddy had made him put on a suit and a tie so a photographer could take our pictures. Daddy was making a big deal out of Neal turning sixteen. I guess because he was old enough to get a driver's license. It certainly wasn't because he was sweet sixteen. Anyway, Neal got the suit all wet when he tripped over his own foot and toppled into the water, so he got to wear his other clothes like he wanted." In a conspiratorial loud whisper, she said, "I think he fell in on purpose."

"Neal?" asked Michele, although she felt she knew the answer by the way Cord had closed his eyes briefly and scowled the first time that the boy's name had been spoken.

Cord made himself look at Michele when Hannah explained, "That's my brother—Neal. He's seventeen now and a pain in the neck."

"I see." Michele slowly raised her eyes from the girl's face to meet Cord's gaze. With difficulty, she asked casually, "Do you have any other brothers or sisters?"

"Nope," the girl said, adding with feeling, "one brother is quite enough, thank you. Especially now that he's nuts about cars since he got his learner's permit."

Michele dropped her gaze. "I can see where that would be a burden."

Hannah volunteered, "Our parents were divorced when I was eight. Daddy went to court to get custody so we could live with him. My mother travels a lot and isn't home much, so they agreed to let Daddy have us with him, but my mother can come to see us whenever she's in town. Daddy says it's important that we have a stable environment.'' She grinned. ''Dumb Neal thought that meant we would live in a stable with horses.''

Cord's mouth twisted in a grimace. The hole he'd dug had just become the Grand Canyon.

Michele smiled faintly. ''You're very lucky to have a father who cares so much for you and your brother.''

''Mom cares about us, too. Daddy says she's a workaholic. That's one of the reasons she and Daddy don't live together anymore. Her business was more important to her than being married.''

''I see,'' murmured Michele. ''How about showing me that boat in the river now?''

Cord couldn't think of anything to say that could erase the devastation lingering in Michele's eyes. His frustration edged his voice when he spoke her name.

''Michele?''

She made a point of looking at her watch and not at him. ''I don't have much time, Cord. Perhaps you should go talk to your partner now. We'll come to the house in about ten minutes, which should give you enough to talk to Mr. Sutherland and clear up a few things before Hannah and I return. Hannah can show me the way.''

''Damn it, Michele,'' he murmured for her ears only.

Meeting his gaze, she said softly, ''Damn you, Cord.''

She walked away from him. Hannah trotted after Michele, oblivious to the tension crackling between the two adults.

It was closer to twenty minutes before Michele asked her half sister to show her where she could find Hannah's father. Her half sister, she repeated silently. The shock of discovery had worn off a little, but the pain that knowledge caused still lingered.

She'd been virtually alone all of her life, with a parent who put her craving for alcohol before the needs of her child. If Michael Sutherland had recognized her as his daughter years ago, her life could have been so different, possibly more normal, probably happier, certainly easier. She would be less than human if she didn't resent the man who could have given her a normal childhood.

Or feel bitter toward the man who had shown her a glimpse of heaven when he'd touched her, then hell when she discovered he had lied to her. Technically, Cord's omission about Michael's other children shouldn't be called a lie, except by omission. But, damn it, she thought, it felt as if he'd been dishonest with her.

Perhaps he'd been lying to her all along about everything, including the attraction he'd implied he felt for her.

It would take some adjustment to accept the existence of a brother and a sister, but she would deal with that later. No matter what it took, she wouldn't let any of them see how devastated she'd felt when she'd learned her father had two other children, two teenagers he'd raised and cared for and loved. She had to get through the next few minutes without losing her composure and her pride.

Or her temper.

Anger had risen to the surface above all her other emotions, threatening to explode at the slightest provocation. But she would contain it. She'd had a lot of practice hiding her emotions. Her whole life, in fact.

Knowing her father had been actively involved in raising Hannah and her brother had been like a slap in the face, and she was still stinging from the blow. But no one else would know. She would make sure of that.

The moment she'd realized who Hannah was, Michele had been determined not to do or say anything to hurt the young girl. It was obvious Hannah was not aware of Michele's relationship to her father. Michele would make sure it stayed that way.

Michael Sutherland's secrecy concerning her wasn't all that surprising, she concluded. Michael had known of her existence and hadn't told his second family he had another child. He evidently only told Cord because he needed his partner to go to Nags Head for him. Cord hadn't been honest with her about vital family details, either. There was no way Michele would be responsible for causing any distress to the young girl or to Hannah's brother, Neal. Her half brother.

Lord, she thought wearily. What a tangled mess.

She was thankful for her professional training, which allowed her to set aside personal feelings in order to get through a difficult situation. She was sometimes so good at suppressing her emotions, she secretly feared ever being able to show her feelings to another person when it mattered. Such as to someone she loved.

Briefly, Cord had made her feel confident of her own femininity, of her desirability, and she'd reveled in the unaccustomed feeling. Her response to him had been overpowering and explosive.

And normal.

Whatever might have been no longer mattered. The devastating sadness that thought created nearly brought her to her knees.

As she did with every other emotion, she tucked her unhappiness deep inside where no one could see it.

During the stroll with Hannah, Michele enjoyed the young girl's chatter, managing to evade most personal questions except the ones about her occupation. Learning that Michele was a veterinarian fascinated Hannah. While showing the river to Michele, Hannah talked about how they'd once had a springer spaniel, but he had been killed by a car last year. Her father had bought flowers to put on the grave Hannah pointed out to Michele, and they'd had an elaborate funeral for their beloved pet.

Michele couldn't help remembering the times she'd buried a pet by herself, tears running down her cheeks as she silently said goodbye to one of her devoted companions. She pushed those thoughts of self-pity aside. Comparing her childhood to Hannah's would only leave her feeling even more desolate than she already felt.

When it was time for them to go inside, Michele went along with Hannah down a wide paneled hallway. She was too apprehensive about meeting Michael Sutherland to notice much about her surroundings beyond a general impression of spaciousness and dark polished wood. Hannah stopped in front of a carved walnut sliding door and rapped lightly.

One of the panels slid open, and Cord stood in the doorway. His gaze flew immediately to Michele's face, a muscle in his jaw clenching when he saw her composed expression. He couldn't find a trace of the generously passionate woman he'd held in his arms on his boat.

But she was there inside the solemn woman in front of him, he knew, and Cord was determined to find her again.

"Hannah," he said to the girl standing next to Michele. "Your father is in his usual chair by the fireplace. Why don't you tell him about your music lesson? I want to talk to Michele for a few minutes, then I'll bring her in to introduce her to your father."

"Okay." Hannah took several steps into the room and turned abruptly to look at Michele. "You won't leave, will you? I'd like to show you my collection of seashells in my room. Maybe you could stay to have dinner with us," she said quickly. "I'll ask Daddy."

"I don't think dinner is a good idea, Hannah, but thank you for inviting me," Michele replied before Cord could. "I can't stay long. I have a long drive back to the Outer Banks."

Hannah tried a different type of coercion. "Persuade her to stay, Uncle Cord. Daddy said you could talk a bird out of the trees, especially if she's a female."

"Michele's not a bird, Hannah. Go say hello to your father. Then trot out to the kitchen and ask Mrs. Trumble to bring coffee in later for Michele and me and a cup of decaf for your father. She could probably round up a glass of milk or juice and a couple of cookies for you while you're in the kitchen. Chew slowly."

"In other words, scram, and take your time coming back," the girl said disgustedly. "I'll be glad when I'm an adult and can stay in the room to hear all the good stuff."

"You're bearing up very well under the strain of being fourteen," he said dryly.

Cord didn't wait to see Hannah go into the study. He took Michele's arm and drew her to the other side of the hallway. His eyes were dark and serious.

"I'm sorry you found out about Hannah and Neal this way, Michele. I didn't intentionally keep them from you."

"It doesn't matter," she said flatly.

His fingers tightened on her arm when she tried to pull away but not enough to cause her any pain.

"It matters, damn it. I don't like knowing I'm responsible for hurting you. I promise to try to never do that again."

Didn't he realize it hurt her just to look at him? she wondered. It was like seeing a beautiful rainbow from a distance and knowing she would never have a chance to find the pot of gold at the end of it.

"I meant we don't need to discuss this now. I'm here to meet Mr. Sutherland, so let's get that over with. Did you talk to him about not telling Hannah and her brother about my relationship to him?"

"Michael agreed not to say anything to Hannah or Neal yet, but he doesn't plan on keeping you a secret for much longer."

Michele didn't like the hesitancy in his voice. It wasn't at all what she'd come to expect from him. Blunt honesty was occasionally a little difficult to take, but he hadn't been timid about speaking until now.

"You might as well say whatever it is you obviously don't want me to know, Cord. Evidently I'm not going to like it, or you wouldn't be pulling your punches."

He debated about adding to her burden when she already had a heavy load to carry. "Michael called his lawyer after I phoned him from the boat. Friedman is coming over right away, so you will be here when Michael makes changes on some legal papers.''

She'd been right. She wasn't going to like what he had to say. "What kind of papers?"

"Something to do with changing his will."

"No. He's not," she stated just before she brushed by him and pushed open the door he'd closed a moment ago.

Her view of the room and the man sitting next to the unlit fireplace had been blocked before by Cord's frame in the doorway. Now she was able to see the man who was listed on her birth certificate as her father.

Even seated in the upholstered chair, he was a large man, full in the chest and shoulders. His hands gripped the arms of the chair as he looked up to gaze at her with piercing green eyes the same color as her own. Dressed in dark slacks and a white shirt with narrow black stripes, he filled the chair, yet Michele doubted if there was an ounce of fat on his tall frame. The only evidence she could see of his recent illness was the pallor of his skin.

Hannah was seated on the footstool in front of his chair, but when she saw Michele, she bounced up and gave her father a peck on the cheek.

"Uncle Cord says I have to make myself scarce, Daddy. Try to get Michele to stay for dinner. I'm always outnumbered with all you guys at the table talking sports and boats and stuff. It'd be fun having another girl to talk to for a change."

His gaze never left Michele's face. "I'll see what I can do, sweetheart. Run along now. I want to talk to Michele."

Hannah nodded and smiled at Michele as she passed her on the way to the door. Reaching Cord, she grinned and said, "I'm going. I'm going."

Cord closed the door after Hannah had left the room and leaned against it, his gaze on Michele's back as she approached Michael's chair. He let his breath out in a rush when he realized he'd been holding it.

Michele walked slowly toward Michael. Stopping several feet away, she smiled faintly. "On the drive here from Nags Head, I tried to think of something clever and witty to say when we met. I couldn't come up with anything then, and I can't now. I suppose saying hello will have to do."

"Hello, Michele," he returned, his voice oddly gruff with emotion. "I can't tell you what it means to see you at last after all these years." He gestured toward a chair, similar to his, placed several feet away. "Won't you sit down?"

"Thank you," she said politely and sat in the chair he'd indicated.

A few moments dragged by in silence. Polite conversation was impossible under the circumstances, and Michael and Michele didn't know each other well enough to take any shortcuts to the subject they both wanted to discuss.

Michele had enough to do absorbing her impressions of the man who was biologically responsible for her existence, without worrying about making social chitchat. Her most powerful sensation was of a devastating disappointment that she didn't feel any sense of familial bond with the man who was technically and legally her father. She realized at that moment how much she had hoped for some sort of connection, but she felt nothing but curiosity.

Michael fell back on small talk, after all. "Cord tells me you have a successful practice as a veterinarian, Michele. How did that come about?"

"Which part?" Without any emotion of any kind, she asked, "Do you want to know how I've developed a successful practice, or why I'm a veterinarian?"

"The choice of veterinarian as a career was a surprise, because I remembered your mother didn't like animals."

Michele thought it was strange how easy the mention of her mother was to him when it shocked her to hear him talk about the woman he divorced.

Realizing he was still waiting for an answer about her choice of career, she said simply, "I've always liked animals."

Michael's smile didn't register in his eyes. Michele sensed he felt the strain of this meeting as much as she did.

"Cord described your clinic, the Sand Dune Animal Hospital, in detail. He even mentioned the Noah's Ark poster in your office and the child's drawing. He was impressed with the professional, caring attitude of your staff. He feels they mirror your own views, that the people who work with you love animals as much as you do."

She didn't acknowledge Cord's presence in the room. "I discovered early that animals were loyal and loving without demanding a great deal except the same from me."

"Many children have pets but don't become veterinarians."

"When I was eight, one of my cats had kittens, but something went wrong. The mother and her kittens died, and I was helpless to do anything about it. I decided then to learn how to heal sick and injured animals."

He nodded, whether in agreement or understanding, Michele had no way of knowing.

"And you worked your way through college by waiting on tables, demonstrating cosmetics in a department store and working in construction. I was somewhat surprised to find out about that last job. Evidently, I'm more old-fashioned than I thought. You look too delicate to be pounding nails with a hammer."

She could mention some of the less-than-ladylike duties she performed as a vet, but she left it alone. "Your private investigator was more thorough than I thought."

Smiling faintly, her father said, "Cord informed me of your reaction to having an investigator poking into your life. I don't blame you for resenting having your privacy invaded, but in my defense, I'd like to state that I tried the obvious means of locating you without success. Since I was looking for Michele Sutherland and not Michele LaBrock, you can understand my difficulties."

The conversation was sliding slowly but inevitably into dangerous territory, and Michele had mixed feelings about venturing into the threatening quicksand created by the past.

"Nothing can be done to change the past. Perhaps we should put it behind us and leave it there."

"I would like nothing better, except there are several misunderstandings that need to be addressed first." Michael glanced at Cord briefly. "Cord told me that your mother led you to believe I was dead. That explains a great deal. Cards I sent were returned un-opened and any present I had delivered was refused at the door. I knew Faith was bitter about the divorce. I was the one who wanted it, you see. She didn't. I won't go into the reasons for wanting out of the marriage except to say there was no other woman involved at the time."

Michele squirmed inwardly. "I don't need to know what happened between you and my mother."

"It's important to me for you to understand that I never forgot you. Even though I stopped child sup-port payments when you turned eighteen, I would have gladly helped you with your college expenses or any-thing else you needed. Unfortunately, you had no way of knowing that."

Michele absorbed this latest shock. "I didn't know you paid child support."

"That doesn't surprise me. I believe you have the impression I walked away and never once looked back. That isn't true. Faith never allowed me to see you, even though legally I was allowed visiting rights. At first, she gave me one excuse after the other every time I called to arrange to see you." He paused for several seconds before continuing, "When she finally said you were afraid of me and didn't want to see me, I stopped pressing."

Michele had to remind herself to control her tem-per. Anger only weakened her, and she needed to be strong. "According to the legal papers Cord showed me, I was only two years old when the divorce was fi-nal. Children that young hate something one minute and love it the next. I don't know the extent of Faith's drinking problem when you were married, but you had to be aware of it even then. Her alcoholism didn't just happen overnight. Yet, you left a two-year-old child with her and believed her when she said that child was afraid of you?''

''You're right, of course. I should have realized she was lying. But you have to believe that I had no idea she was an alcoholic. She would have a few drinks in the evenings and occasionally drink too much. I honestly did not realize the extent of her abuse of alcohol.''

Michele's earliest memory was the cloying sweet smell of whiskey. How could he not have seen Faith's dependency on booze? she wondered.

''I'm not trying to put all the blame on your mother,'' he explained. ''At the time, I was starting a new life and decided to let you get on with yours without being pulled back and forth between us.'' He paused, then he said, ''But all that is in the past. It's the future I wish to discuss with you now. I don't like your request to keep our relationship a secret.''

''Mr. Sutherland,'' she began with a hint of impatience, surprised when he flinched at the formal use of his name. ''I've met Hannah. She's a happy, secure, sweet child. Let's allow her to stay that way. Neither she nor her brother need to have their lives disrupted, and they would be if they were exposed to the skeleton in the family closet.''

''You make it sound as though your relationship to this family is an embarrassment.''

Michele, for once, let her silence speak for her.

Michael's mouth twisted in a grimace. ''Lord knows, I neglected my duty toward you as you were growing up, but I wish to correct that now. I've asked my lawyer here today so you can read my will, which lists you along with Hannah and Neal as my beneficiaries. I made that provision long before I knew you thought I was dead. It's a small consolation, I realize, but I have always acknowledged our relationship legally."

"You put me in your will," she commented. "Which means I would have had one hell of a shock when your lawyer contacted me to tell me the father I thought was already dead had just died and left me money. That would have been such a comfort."

A slight flush put color into his pale cheeks. "I don't blame you for being bitter, Michele. I have handled this badly, but it's not too late to do something to correct the situation."

"There is no situation to correct. I have no complaints, so you needn't feel guilty. I also don't want your money. Your children are your rightful heirs."

"You are my oldest child." When she didn't say anything, Michael said, "I want you to become a real member of this family, Michele. It's not too late for you to take your rightful position as my daughter." He hesitated for ten seconds, then plunged ahead. "I want your permission to put you down as co-guardian to Hannah and Neal if anything happens to their mother after I'm gone. My ex-wife, Pilar, travels a great deal because of her job and the odds are greater that something could happen to her than if she remained in one place."

What little color was left in Michele's face completely washed away. Finding it suddenly difficult to catch her breath, she leaned back in the chair and fought to maintain control. She felt a slight weight on her shoulder and realized Cord was standing behind her chair and had placed his hand on her shoulder.

Panic welled up inside her and she got to her feet, barely resisting the urge to run out of the room.

"Who do you have listed as their guardian now?" she asked quietly, surprised that she could speak. It was a silly question, anyway. She already knew the answer.

Her father's gaze rose to the man standing behind the chair she'd just vacated. "Cord has known Hannah and Neal for the last ten years, and he will have my share of the business to help provide for them. He's agreed to my wish to sign my half of the business over to you in case of Pilar's death and mine, so you would be financially able to care for Hannah and Neal with Cord. I realize this isn't a pleasant topic of conversation to bring up the first time we meet, and if I hadn't recently had a heart attack, I wouldn't have thought it was necessary. Under the circumstances, though, it's important to me to get these matters settled."

Michele clutched at the strap of her purse as if it were a lifeline and she was in danger of drowning. She felt as though she were being carried away by a strong undertow of responsibility that threatened to hold her under until she suffocated. The burden of caring for her mother was heavy enough. She didn't need or want the added weight of two teenagers who were complete strangers. She knew nothing about real family life.

"You can't do this to your children. They don't even know me. How would they feel once they find out about my real relationship to them, one that's been kept hidden from them like some deep dark secret?"

"They will understand. They are both well-adjusted youngsters who will accept you without question."

"Please, leave everything the way it is. Your children should have the security of their own home and will need their close relationship with Cord if anything happens to you and their mother."

"And you, Michele? What will you have?" he asked quietly.

"What I've always had," she murmured with a hint of defiance. "Myself, my work and animals. I also have enough responsibility taking care of Faith, Mr. Sutherland. Your children will be better off with Cord."

Cord stepped around the chair and put his hand on Michael's forearm, his gaze on his partner's pale face.

"Discuss all of this at another time, Michael. You've had enough excitement for one day."

Impatiently brushing off Cord's concern, Michael said, "I'm all right." He looked at his daughter, who had walked to the door prepared to leave. "For what it's worth, Michele, I am sorry about the past. Perhaps I don't deserve your generosity, but I would greatly appreciate getting to know you and have you become better acquainted with me and your brother and sister. I regret that it's taken the jolt of a heart attack to remind me of what's important in life, and that is family. Please come to see me again."

Michele turned slowly and met his gaze, "I'm sorry my visit has upset you. That wasn't my intention. If I do come to visit you again, it will only be as a friend of the family, not as a member of it. Anything else wouldn't be fair to your children."

"You are my child, too, Michele," her father pointed out.

A corner of her mouth lifted in a self-deprecating smile. "Give me a little time to get used to that fact.

You've had twenty-eight years. I've had less than a week to get used to having a father."

"That's the problem," Michael said with a trace of despair. "I'm not sure how much time I have left."

"I've learned not to depend on anyone else to solve my problems or to complete my life. You can't lose what you've never had, Mr. Sutherland. Concentrate on getting well, for your own sake and for your children."

Both men stared at her retreating figure. The sound of the door closing quietly after her seemed final and binding.

Chapter Ten

By the time Cord got to the front door, Michele's car was at the end of the driveway, turning onto the road. A few seconds later, her car was out of sight.

"Damn it," he cursed softly.

This thing with Michele was tangled up more than any backlashed fishing reel he'd ever seen. When he ended up with one of those, he usually cut his losses and started over with fresh line. He didn't know what in hell he was going to do about this snarled situation.

Returning to Michael's study, Cord saw him slip a small white tablet under his tongue. The older man seemed paler than before, and he was perspiring. Fear coiled in Cord's stomach.

"Michael? Are you all right? Is it your heart?"

"Calm down, Cord. My ticker is racing a little fast, that's all."

"So is mine." Cord sat down in the chair Michele had recently vacated. "I take back every nasty thing I ever said about your being pigheaded, Michael. Your daughter has you beat hands down in the stubborn department."

"My daughter," repeated Michael as though trying out the word. He rested his head on the high padded back of his chair. "I've really made a mess of things, Cord."

Sitting in the chair Michele had occupied had been a mistake, Cord realized too late. The cushion was still warm from her body, and his own body reacted. "I haven't exactly racked up a lot of points, either."

Michael closed his eyes briefly. "The investigator gave me the facts but not the emotions behind them. Why did I think this was going to be so easy? I stupidly thought all I had to do was say I was sorry to her, to ask her to forgive me for leaving her with an alcoholic mother—and by the way, would she help take care of my other children for me, the ones I raised while she was trying to keep her mother out of bars?"

"You wanted this meeting to work out, Michael. There's no crime in that. You can't expect an instant reconciliation. Give it some time. Give her time."

Opening his eyes, Michael looked at Cord. "It's been worse for her than the investigator led us to believe, hasn't it?"

"I'm afraid so. She doesn't talk about her mother much, but from what I gathered from the bartender and her own actions the night we went looking for Faith, Michele has been taking care of her mother for a long time, probably most of her life. I have a feeling that's the way it's been since Michele was old enough to walk and talk."

"From the time she was two years old and she was left alone with Faith, is what you're trying to say."

"They are the facts, Michael. There's nothing either of us can do to change them."

"And she won't allow me to do anything about her future. I wanted to make it up to her for neglecting her all those years, but she doesn't want anything from me."

"Not your money anyway. What she needs, she won't allow you to give her. Or me, either, after today," Cord said pensively.

Michael looked at Cord intently. Leaning forward in his chair, he asked, "What does she need? If it's even remotely possible, I'll see that she gets it."

Cord shook his head. "It can't be bought, only given. Animals have been her sole source most of her life."

"Love," murmured Michael, settling back in his chair.

"Love," confirmed Cord. "I've never known anyone who needs love more than she does."

His partner stared at Cord long and hard. Finally, he said softly, "I'll be damned. Cynical Captain Cord Thomas has fallen overboard for my daughter."

With a grimace twisting his mouth, Cord muttered, "'Don't get your shorts in a bunch,' as Rocky used to say. I don't know what the hell I feel for her except I want her." His frown turned into a scowl. "This is the damnedest conversation to be having with the father of the woman I want to take to bed."

Michael grinned. "For what it's worth, you have my blessing."

"Gee, thanks," Cord drawled. His attention shifted to the view through the window, but he was looking farther away in his mind. "I'm going to take a couple of days off. Everything is running smoothly at the restaurants. The marina can page me if something comes up."

"Going someplace?" Michael asked with exaggerated innocence.

"Yeah, either to heaven or to hell. It's going to be up to Michele." He looked at his partner. "I can't make any promises, Michael. If she wants any type of relationship with either one of us, it has to be up to her."

"I understand."

Cord stood. "She's a very compassionate woman, Michael. She'll be back."

"I hope you're right."

Cord also hoped he was right. He was very much afraid his life wouldn't be complete unless Michele was in it.

Michele leaned back against the kitchen cupboard door and shifted her hips to try to find a more comfortable position on the hard linoleum floor. She didn't find it. A tingling sensation in her right foot warned her that it was falling asleep. Unless she wanted a numb foot, she was going to have to rearrange the sleeping puppies on her lap.

That was easier than it sounded, she realized. Both of her arms were full with a puppy tucked into each side; two puppies were sprawled across one thigh, and another was precariously balanced between both of her legs.

She had no one to blame but herself for being in this predicament. Her receptionist Gail's daughter would have continued caring for the anemic puppies someone had left on Michele's doorstep, just as she had during the week and yesterday. But Michele had used the excuse of giving Opal a break when she'd stopped by to pick them up after her return from Virginia Beach yesterday. Michele would have to take them back to her on her way to the clinic on Monday morning so Opal could continue administering their special feedings.

The real reason Michele had fetched the puppies was that she wanted their company for the weekend. Some women shopped when they needed cheering up. She knew a few who made an appointment to get a facial and their hair styled. Her friend and neighbor Barbara went jogging when she had a problem to solve. Michele sought out an animal needing special attention and care.

After feeding the puppies the special formula early Sunday evening, she'd remained on the floor with them, enjoying their antics as they crawled over her. She always received a great deal of satisfaction from seeing an animal recover from a serious illness, knowing she was partly responsible for saving its life.

Her mind had drifted to the meeting with her father, and before she realized it, the puppies with their full tummies had fallen asleep where they lay. Which happened to be on her.

If it wasn't for her foot going to sleep, she would have been willing to stay where she was for a while. The sound of the rain beating against the window above the sink made her feel lonely and melancholy, and the warmth of the little furry bodies was comforting.

It wouldn't be the first time she'd used animals to fight loneliness. There had been many occasions in her life when a dog or cat had provided company and affection during long nights and empty days. Somehow the nights didn't appear as dark or as frightening when she had a cat to hold or a dog lying across her feet.

Her mouth twisted ruefully. Tonight wouldn't be the first or the last time she depended on animals to fight suffocating depression.

The unexpected sound of someone knocking on her front door had her frowning. Turning her wrist enough to read her watch, she saw that it was only eight o'clock in the evening, not all that late for someone to be out and about. Except she rarely had visitors at this hour since Barbara had flown to England two weeks ago on vacation.

Whoever it was, he or she was becoming impatient. The earlier tap was followed by several louder knocks.

Michele eased the sleeping puppies onto her lap so her hands were free to lift each one into the shallow wicker basket on the floor next to her. The last puppy began to whimper when she lifted him. Michele tucked him into her bent arm and took him with her to the door. As much as she enjoyed their company, she didn't want all the puppies awake again until she had dealt with whoever was at the door.

Turnip and Aristotle, two older mixed-breed dogs, left their cozy positions near the fireplace to accompany her to the door. Their lack of enthusiasm was obvious by the faint wag of tails and unhurried stroll.

"I appreciate the thought, guys, but I can handle this one. Go back to your places by the fire."

Both dogs turned in tandem and plodded back to the fireplace.

She chuckled. "I feel so safe knowing you two are here to protect me."

She was still smiling when she opened the door.

A jagged streak of lightning cracked across the sky as she opened the door, briefly illuminating the figure standing on her front porch. Her smile faded.

"Cord!"

"Who were you talking to?"

"My dogs. What are you doing here?"

"I'm getting wet at the moment."

She stepped aside so he could enter. "You'd better come in, then."

Crossing the threshold, he began to shuck off his wet nylon jacket after closing the door behind him. Underneath, his dark green shirt was dry, although spots of rain dotted the thighs of his jeans.

He saw the puppy tucked up against her side. "This is the second time I've wished I was a dog."

Michele blinked in surprise. "Why would you want to be a dog?"

"They manage to get closer to you than I do. The first time was when our friend Willoughby managed to get up close and personal."

As if on cue, the puppy whined softly and pressed his damp nose into her side, only inches from the tip of her breast. The white cotton T-shirt she wore wasn't much of a defense against the animal's cold nose, and Michele flinched.

She hadn't been expecting company and had dressed in her usual at-home attire: a cotton T-shirt without a bra and well-worn jeans. The puppy's movements caused the material to pull tighter over her breast, eliminating any need for Cord to guess what she might be wearing under the shirt.

Michele turned away. "I'll go put him down with the others."

She didn't wait for Cord to agree or disagree. He didn't do either one. He came with her.

In the kitchen, Michele knelt down and carefully placed the puppy in the basket with the others who thankfully were still sleeping.

The last puppy didn't miss the warmth of Michele's body once he was nestled between two of his siblings. He made a muffled grunting sound and settled in.

Michele automatically stroked the back of a finger across each warm little body before she straightened, nearly bumping into Cord, who was behind her looking into the basket.

"Cute," he said softly, reaching out to prevent her from backing away from him.

"And noisy when they're awake," she whispered. "So we'd better go into the other room."

In the living room, she gestured toward the cushioned rattan couch and two matching chairs arranged around a freestanding fireplace almost in the center of the room.

"If you'd like to sit down, you'll have to step around the dogs. They claim squatter's rights whenever I make a fire."

Cord gazed down at the dogs sprawled on the floor. "So they are actually alive?"

"They save their energy for really important things like dinner."

"I suppose I should have expected you to have animals at home. How many more are there?"

"Two cats, Coco and Max. You won't see Max. He doesn't like people much. Coco will be in my bedroom. He has claimed my bed as his own personal property." She pointed to the wine-colored bundle of fur first. "This is Turnip and the other one is Aristotle."

Cord's gaze went from the dogs to the circular fireplace. He could see flickering flames through a black mesh screen. It wasn't a raging fire like Rocky used to make on the beach when Cord was a kid, but a gentle blaze that gave off aesthetic warmth along with the natural heat from the flames.

Behind him, Michele asked, "Are you going to sit down or are you just passing through?"

He would like to do a lot of things, but he would start by accepting the only invitation she'd given him. It was more than he'd expected from her after their last meeting.

He chose one of the chairs and sank down onto the flowery print cushion. Stretching his long legs out toward the fire, he stared into the flames. "Nice fire."

Michele tucked one leg under her and sat down at one end of the couch. "I like it. Why are you here, Cord?"

He raised his gaze from the fire, and she discovered a different heat burning in his eyes as he looked at her. "You were supposed to go back to the boat yesterday after you saw Michael. We were going to talk, remember?"

"I was about all talked out after meeting Mr. Sutherland."

"Why do you find it so hard to refer to Michael as your father, Michele? Not saying it doesn't make it any less true."

"But saying the words somehow make the relationship more real, and he's a stranger." She leaned forward. "He hasn't taken a turn for the worse after my visit, has he?"

"His guilt is giving him more pain than his heart."

Settling back in her seat, Michele said, "Including me in his will isn't the way to make up for the past. It isn't necessary."

"I don't want to talk about Michael or Hannah or Neal or your mother. Not tonight. I came here to talk about you and me."

Her breath hitched in her throat. "I don't see how we can just ignore them, Cord."

"We can't ignore this attraction that makes us so aware of each other, either. It doesn't change anything when you try to deny it," he added when she shook her head. "I wasn't the only one involved in that kiss on the boat."

Too restless to sit calmly and discuss how she'd responded to him, Michele uncurled from the couch and got to her feet. She walked over to the window and watched the rain trickle down the glass, wrapping her arms around her waist to ward off the chill in the air now that she was away from the fire. Her gaze settled on a small raindrop that gathered speed and volume as it ran into other dots of water along the way to the bottom of the pane of glass. Her situation with Cord and Michael was very similar, she thought, gaining weight and momentum with every passing day.

"Maybe we should leave things the way they are without complicating both our lives," she said quietly.

Cord saw his image reflected in the glass when he approached her from behind. He could make out her features enough to notice she hadn't withdrawn into her protective shell as he'd expected.

He placed his hands on her shoulders and met her gaze in the glass. "I vowed after my divorce I would never get involved with anyone ever again. I kept that promise until the day I met you. Now I'm so damn swamped with thoughts of you, with wanting you, I can't think straight.''

"Evidently I've given you the wrong impression about me. I don't go in for one-night stands.''

"Evidently I've given you the wrong impression about what I want from you,'' he said with a slow smile. His fingers moved caressingly on the fine bones under his hands. "One night won't be enough, Michele.''

She turned, relieved when he lifted his hands, but her relief was brief. Once she was facing him, he brought his hands back to her shoulders, his hold even more possessive than before.

It should have been easy to tell him she wasn't interested in him. She could say the words, but she wouldn't mean them.

"This might sound like a lame excuse,'' she said softly. "But I'm only trying to save us both some trouble, Cord.''

"Honey, you've been nothing but trouble since I met you,'' he said with a small smile. "I'm still coming back for more, so that should tell you something.''

"It tells me you're an incredibly stubborn man who is used to getting what he wants,'' she said with a hint of tolerant amusement. "What I'm trying to tell you is that I'm not sure I have anything to give you.''

"I don't know if I do, either, but I'm willing to try. That's all I'm asking you to do.'' He moved his hands closer to her throat, his thumbs stroking her skin. "Neither one of us has had the kind of backgrounds that makes for great relationship material. I got dumped when I was twelve by a mother who didn't give a damn about me and was divorced by a wife-in-name-only. You were abandoned by your father when you were two and lived with a woman who cared only where her next drink was coming from. We would both be starting from the same place, which puts us on equal ground. I like the way I feel when I'm with you, Michele, and I don't want to lose that. I have no idea where this is going, but I'm willing to take the first step to get there.''

Overwhelmed by his honesty, Michele let her head fall forward until her forehead was resting on his chest. "Couldn't you just throw me over your shoulder and carry me into the bedroom and have your wicked way with me?''

He surprised them both by chuckling. Then he placed a bent finger under her chin to force her to look at him. "Believe me, honey, the thought has crossed my mind once or twice. The problem with the caveman approach would be that I wouldn't know if you wanted me as much as I wanted you. There's a big difference between making love *to* you and making love *with* you. I want you with me the whole way or it won't be any good for either of us.''

A delicious warmth flowed over her at the thought of his body melding with hers. "The puppies have to be fed again in two hours.''

Cord's body tightened in anticipation. "That might be just enough time.''

Knowing she wanted him created a fierce male response that made his hands tremble slightly as he reached for her. His hunger fought with his control as he lowered his head to take her mouth. A surge of desire rushed through him like a flaming rocket when her lips parted in silent invitation. She wanted him!

Michele wanted to touch him, to give him a little of the pleasure he gave her when his hands moved over her. Her fingers worked on the buttons down the front of his shirt as he slanted his mouth over hers to give him greater access to her moist warmth. The pleasure was so intense, the arousal so strong, she almost forgot her original intention to open his shirt—until her fingers came in contact with the crisp hair on his chest.

A thrill of feminine triumph blended with all the other feelings he created in her when she heard him groan as her fingers brushed across a sensitive nipple.

Cord broke away from her mouth and buried his face in her hair, taking in the scent of her along with badly needed air. "I'm not going to last very long at this rate."

She touched her lips to his throat. "If you stop now, I'll toss you out into the rain."

He chuckled. "It would be easier to stop breathing."

Suddenly she felt the room spin around her and realized he'd picked her up in his arms. "I thought they only did this in the movies," she murmured as she wrapped her arms around his neck.

"On certain occasions, it's appropriate in real life when a man needs to get a woman to a bed before he goes crazy."

The door to her bedroom was open, revealing her double bed covered with a dark floral spread. Something flashed past his foot when he walked toward the bed.

"What was that?"

"Was it tan-and-white?" she murmured as she left a moist trail of kisses on his throat.

"How would I know? It went by too fast."

"It was probably Coco. He sleeps on my bed."

Cord released her legs slowly and enjoyed the feel of her thighs brushing his until she was standing in front of him. So close but not close enough. Bending his head, he left a scorching path of kisses along the slender lines of her jaw and throat.

"How does Coco feel about someone being in your bed with you?"

"I don't know. There's never been anyone else in this bed."

Cord raised his head to look at her, his gray eyes wide with shock. "Never? You mean . . . ?"

"I'm not a virgin, if that's what you want to know. It happened when I was in college. Only once, and it wasn't very successful. He thought so, too, and forgot he'd sworn his undying love forever and ever. I never saw him again. I haven't been anxious to repeat the performance."

"Until now?"

She met his gaze. "Until you."

His senses reeled with the knowledge that she wanted him enough to put aside her reservations. Her admission explained part of the reason she had been reluctant to go to bed with him, but also how much she had to overcome in her mind before giving herself to him. Knowing she wanted him in spite of everything was as arousing as touching her. He was more determined than ever to show her how good they would be together. He didn't share her doubts that making love with her would be like any other experience either one of them had ever had.

He gave in to the fantasy he'd had ever since the first time he'd seen her, when the Yorkshire terrier had burrowed against her breasts. With his hands at her waist, he lifted her up far enough for him to bury his face in the space between her breasts. He felt her tremble and turned his head to take the tip of her breast into his mouth. Even through the material of her cotton top, he could feel the hard bud blossom against his lips. As much as he wanted to continue torturing himself with the feel and taste of her, his whole body was surging with fevered arousal that couldn't be denied much longer.

Michele swayed against him when he took her mouth again. She made a sound of protest when he moved away from her in order to make room to lift her shirt over her head. Then his hands were covering her bare breasts, and she made a different sound deep in her throat. Her yearning sigh struck a responding chord deep inside him, and Cord knew the waiting was over.

With a small part of his mind that could still register something other than his desire for her, Cord realized with amazement that his fingers weren't steady when he slid his hand down her rib cage to the fastener of her jeans. He swept away the remainder of her clothing, including orange socks with black butterflies on them that made him smile. He tore back the covers on the bed before laying her down on the white sheets.

His gaze roamed over her body as though committing the sight of her slender curves to memory as he stood beside her bed and stripped off his clothing. He searched her eyes for any sign of doubt or fear, seeing only a dazed need and burning arousal.

As badly as he wanted to join his body with hers, he somehow managed to find enough sanity to remember the necessity of protecting her. It seemed forever but was actually only a few seconds before he bent his knee and leaned over her. His eyes never left hers. Her eyes were the mirror of her soul and the only sure way he had of knowing she had no doubts about giving herself to him.

Her lips curved slowly into a smile as old as time as she raised her arms in silent invitation.

He thought he would shatter with the pleasure soaring through him when he felt her soft slender body under his. He took her mouth with barely suppressed control as he slid his hand between them to test her readiness. When her hips arched into his hand, he wrapped his arms around her and forged deeply inside her.

An exquisite sigh of aching pleasure escaped Michele's parted lips, and he claimed her mouth with fevered possession. He tried to give her time to adjust to him, but when she drew her legs up alongside his, the motion drew him deeper inside, and he lost the slim hold on his control.

A coiling tension began to tighten and twist as he moved against her, then with her as she instinctively matched his fierce desire. Lightning flashed outside the bedroom and thunder vibrated through the air, an explosive background for the storm brewing deep inside their bodies.

Michele gasped his name as tremors shook her violently. Her response triggered his own, and he joined her in a pulsating release that left him feeling fulfilled in a way he couldn't possibly describe to her or even to himself.

Cord buried his face in the hollow of her throat and felt her arms holding him securely as they rode out the aftershocks. His name drifted to him in a whispered sigh as soft as a gentle breeze. Her warm breath against her skin was almost as satisfying as the feel of her breasts pressed against his chest.

When his mind began to function normally again, he thought of her comfort. He was too heavy for her and reluctantly rolled onto his side to ease his weight off her. She made a sound of protest, which he soothed by leaning on his elbow to kiss her lingeringly.

The wind outside blew a handful of sand across the closed window, then washed it away with a sheet of rain. Cord realized the air in the room was cool on his heated body. Reaching down, he retrieved a sheet and a quilt from the foot of the bed and brought it up to cover their damp bodies.

He slid his arm around Michele to bring her against his side as he lay on his back and stared up at the ceiling. Her hair brushed over his skin like strands of silk when she laid her head on his shoulder. Her hand rested on his chest, and he covered it with his. She sighed contentedly, and Cord smiled.

A feeling unlike anything he'd ever felt before stole over him. He suddenly realized what it was. For the first time in memory, he felt at peace with himself and the world around him. It was as though all the separate pieces that made up the diverse aspects of his life had magically fallen into place.

And it wasn't just physical satisfaction. Although, Lord knows, that was certainly part of it.

The cause of this incredible contentment was the woman he was holding securely in his arms.

Michele gently moved her fingers in the crisp curling hairs on his chest, enjoying the feel of the solid muscles underneath her hand. She savored the lack of self-consciousness she thought she would be feeling. She was lying beside a naked man she'd known for a very short time, yet she wasn't ashamed or embarrassed. Why was that? she wondered.

She knew only that being with Cord like this felt right, as though he were the missing link in the chain of her existence. For the first time in memory, the suffocating fog of loneliness had dissipated from around her, replaced by an odd sensation she could only label contentment. Before she'd met Cord, she'd felt incomplete, she realized, and now she was whole. How long this feeling would last she had no way of knowing. All she could do was to hold on to it as long as she could.

She had no illusions it would last.

She pushed away the niggling thought that crept into her mind, whispering a warning for her to count on only tonight, this moment with Cord. Forever was a long time. And unknown. There was only now.

Cord rolled partially on his side toward her so he could reach under him to find whatever was pressing into his hip. His fingers closed around a small object, and he brought it around his body so he could examine it.

He wasn't any wiser when he saw it. "What is this?"

Michele raised her head to see what he was holding. "That's Coco's catnip mouse."

"What do I do with it?"

"Toss it onto the floor. He'll find it." Michele brought both her hands onto his chest and rested her chin on them. "Are you staying the night?" she asked.

"Am I invited?"

Without hesitation, Michele said, "Yes."

"Rocky used to say if a man doesn't have the sense to get in out of the rain, he doesn't have the brain God gave a goose." He hugged her closer. "No one's going to call me stupid. I'll stay right here."

"You cleaned up the quote from Rocky."

He chuckled. "He drilled it home to me not to cuss in front of ladies."

She moved her fingers on his chest, enjoying the freedom to touch him. "Tell me about Rocky."

He took a deep, relaxing breath. The rain was clattering against the window and the wind was picking up in intensity. Michele was warm and soft in his arms.

His voice was low in the dark intimacy of night. "When I ran away from the shopping center, I had no idea where I was or where I was going to go. The mall wasn't the one we usually went to. I just kept walking until it got dark and I was too tired to go any farther. Somehow I'd ended up at Rudee Inlet, where a bunch of boats were tied up. I climbed aboard one and fell asleep on some canvas folded and piled in a corner of the deck."

Michele wanted to see his face, so she propped herself up on her elbow. "Was it Rocky's boat?"

He nodded. "Not the one I live on. It was a smaller boat, a thirty-footer." He reached up to tuck a strand of her hair behind her ear. "When I woke up the next morning, this gruff voice told me to get my butt in gear. I wouldn't get breakfast until I swabbed the deck."

"Which you did."

"Darn right. I was hungry. Rocky asked me my name, told me to call him Rocky and held out his hand. I shook it, he handed me a fishing reel and a spool of line and showed me how to fill the reel. From then on, I learned to crew on weekends and during the summers when I didn't go to school. I lived with Rocky from that day until I got married.''

''He took you in, just like that?''

''He took me on as a crew member after asking me if I had anywhere else to go. Later he told me he had been impressed when I hadn't whined or cried when I told him my mother had dumped me at a mall. I found out years afterward that he'd been an orphan. He understood what it felt like not to have anybody care what happened to you.''

''It's possible something could have happened to your mother that prevented her from returning for you. She might have had an accident or become too ill to tell anyone where she'd left you.''

''Rocky had a friend on the police force check hospital emergency rooms and missing person reports. Neither my mother's name nor mine were found on either one. She'd vacated our apartment owing rent, taking her own clothes but leaving my stuff behind.''

''Did you ever try to find her?''

''No,'' he said flatly. ''What would be the point?''

Michele lay quietly beside him, thinking about Cord's childhood. His hadn't been any more normal than hers. Maybe, she thought, a so-called normal childhood was a myth. Each person was raised differently and not necessarily like the images in a Norman Rockwell painting.

His fingers slid into her hair. ''I can practically hear your brain clicking away. What are you thinking about?''

Her fingers stroked soothingly across his chest, but the motion didn't soothe either one of them.

"I was comparing my childhood to yours. Perhaps we wouldn't be the people we are today if we'd had different experiences."

"I don't have any regrets." He rolled over and pushed her onto her back. "I certainly have no complaints about where I've ended up."

She hooked her arms around his neck as he parted her legs and made a place for himself between them.

"Who's complaining?' she murmured just before he covered her mouth with his.

Chapter Eleven

Michele was accustomed to waking up with the weight of her twelve-pound cat lying on her chest in the morning. A one-hundred-eighty-pound man partially covering her was definitely an unusual event.

She opened her eyes. Cord's gray eyes were gazing down at her with heated desire burning in their depths. She raised her arms to slip around him as he lowered his head. His kiss drew her immediately into the blatantly sensual pool of need and passion.

"Cord," she murmured against his throat.

Desire made his hands and mouth greedy, and he filled himself with her scent and taste.

"Say my name again," he said raggedly.

"Cord..." she said with a sigh, his name trailing off when she caught her breath as he moved his hand to her damp center. "Cord!" she cried out.

He had wanted her before he was fully awake. Now he craved her, needed her more than his next breath. In some small part of his mind, he knew he always would. He felt the bite of her fingernails on his back and his body pulsed with a desperate hunger to mate with the woman who had been created just for him.

He held her hips in his hands and filled her slowly and deeply. The pleasure shuddered through him into her, and he took her involuntary cry of sweet agony into his mouth.

The past and the future ceased to exist. There was only now. And each other.

Cord locked her to him as the culmination of their matched desire rippled through them simultaneously. He murmured her name as though she was his soul and his salvation. He was beginning to recognize that she was both.

A long time later, he took a deep breath and slowly, reluctantly, rolled onto his side. Michele made a sound of protest and moved with him.

As much as he liked the thought of never being separated from her again, he had to or they would never leave the bed.

"Honey, if we stay like this, those puppies will starve, and we'll waste away to nothing after making love continually for days."

She scrunched up her brow as she pretended to give what he said serious thought.

Cord chuckled and lifted her hips away from his while he still could without wanting her again. "Don't we need to feed the puppies?"

"You slept through one of their feedings." She glanced at the bedside clock as the digital numbers changed to 5:55 in the morning. "They'll be waking up soon." She leaned on her elbow so she could see him. She never tired of looking at his strong features. Even when he needed a shave.

"I meant what I said to Michael Sutherland. I don't want him to change his previous arrangements. I don't want him to include me in his will."

Cord blinked in surprise at the abrupt statement. "I thought you didn't want to talk about him."

"I don't, but we have to discuss it sometime." She didn't want to remind him or herself that this might be the only time they had. "It might as well be now."

Cord adjusted the pillow under his head to a more comfortable position. "Michael feels guilty for all the years he stayed out of your life. He wants to make it up to you by including you in his second family."

"Having me crammed down their throats isn't the way to persuade them to accept me. They know you. It wouldn't be fair to make them take in someone who's a stranger to them if they do lose their father and mother. I saw Hannah's face light up when she first saw you. You've been an important part of her life for a long time. I haven't met her brother, but I imagine he feels the same way or Sutherland wouldn't have chosen you to be their guardian. If anything does happen, the children will have enough adjustments to make without having to deal with a virtual stranger."

"He's hoping to change that."

"Change what?"

"The fact that you're a stranger to the kids. He wants you to become a recognized member of the family."

Levering herself up to a sitting position, Michele drew the sheet up to cover her breasts, feeling suddenly vulnerable and exposed. She bit her bottom lip and looked toward the window rather than meet his eyes.

"Michele?"

She didn't realize her expression had changed until he growled, "Damn it, don't do that!"

Startled by the anger in his voice, she jerked her head around to look at him. "Do what?"

"Withdraw behind that steel curtain you erect like a shield."

Puzzled, she stared at him. "What are you talking about?"

"You aren't even aware you do it, are you?"

"Do what?"

"You draw back like a turtle into his shell faster than a gunfighter could pull out his gun. Now that I know you better, I'm beginning to understand why you use it as a way of protecting yourself, but you don't need to do that around me. Talk to me, damn it. If we're to have any hope for a relationship of any kind, you can't keep shutting me out."

Knowing he was right didn't make it any easier to put her fears into words. "It's not easy for me to share my feelings."

"I didn't say it would be easy. I want you to trust me with more than your body. I want to understand why you withdraw inside yourself."

She tried to think rationally and clearly how she could explain the reason for her reserved nature so he would understand.

"There's a certain degree of shame in having a parent who drinks heavily that I don't think ever goes away when a child has been exposed to it at an early age. The perceptions might change and dull with time but they never fade completely. It's like a family secret that is kept hidden from outsiders so the skeleton in the closet isn't exposed to anyone else. If you try to look at it logically, it doesn't make much sense, but counselors I've talked to say it's a normal reaction for children of alcoholics."

Cord shifted his long body to a sitting position and leaned back against the headboard. "No kid wants to admit his parent is less than perfect. I used to make up some elaborate stories about where my parents were. Having them be missionaries in some unheard-of tropical island was preferable to telling other kids that I never knew my father and that my mother neglected to come back for me one day."

Michele wondered how extensive the damage being abandoned had done to Cord's ability to trust people. She recognized the symptoms because she had the same problem. For the first time in her life, she had taken the chance of sharing her thoughts with someone else and he had understood.

"As you know, my mother has denied that her ex-husband is even alive. I don't know how she rationalized receiving monthly child support checks when she considered him dead, but I believe she told that lie so often, she convinced herself it was true. It wouldn't have been the first one."

Cord watched her intently, his gaze straining to catch every nuance of expression in the dimly lighted bedroom. "Are you afraid if you get involved with your father and his family against her wishes, your mother might go off the deep end?"

"It's more than just a possibility. All I did was mention his name the night after you came to the clinic the first time, and she tried to drink Nags Head dry."

"You aren't taking the blame for that, are you?"

She shrugged. "Intellectually, no. She's responsible for her own actions. But there's a little voice inside me that says if I hadn't mentioned his name, she wouldn't have gone off that night. A cocktail waitress at one of the hotels brought Faith home after the bar closed. Mrs. Walcott found her passed out in the front seat of her car the next morning."

"I take it your mother doesn't know about the little trip to Virginia Beach yesterday."

She shook her head. "I didn't tell her, and I asked Mrs. Walcott not to say anything about where I'd gone. Faith would consider my seeing Michael Sutherland as an act of betrayal if she knew I met him. I don't know what she would do under those circumstances, but I can guarantee I wouldn't like it. Her reactions are usually self-destructive."

Cord took her hand, not all that surprised to find her fingers were cold. "She was the one who made the decision to keep you isolated from your father by telling you he was dead. She apparently took his money for child support without any qualms. Keeping your father from you was an even bigger act of betrayal on her part."

She gazed at him with shock in the depths of her eyes. "I never thought of it that way."

He cupped his hand around her neck, feeling the tension under his fingers. "That's because you're so used to looking at things from her perspective, you don't look at them from your own. You have a life, too, Michele. It's not fair to you to have to live it according to your mother's actions. Until she admits she has a problem and gets some help, it sounds like she's going to drink whether you give her a reason or not."

"I know." She sighed heavily. "I've lost count of how many different professionals I've seen to try to find a solution, to get her to stop." Her voice quivered slightly when she added, "I hate it when she drinks."

"And her?" he asked softly. "How do you feel about her when she's been drinking?"

"I feel sorry for her."

"Michele," he prodded gently. "Tell me how you really feel about your mother when she's drunk—when you have to clean up after her, when you have to enter bar after bar looking for her, when you have to buy back things she's pawned for enough money for a drink?"

She looked at him with a haunting sadness in her eyes. "Don't make me say it."

"I'm not going to force you to say or do anything, Michele. Ever. But you need to admit how you feel aloud or the hate will fester inside you."

Her image of him was blurred by the tears welling up in her eyes. "I hate her drinking," she said hoarsely. "Yet I love her and I'm ashamed, humiliated and angry with her most of the time. She hasn't always been like she is today. There were times when she used to laugh and play silly games with me. I hate the waste of her talent, her intelligence, her spirit, all of those things drowned by the disease of alcoholism. I hate knowing I can save an animal's life, but I can't save hers." -

Cord reached for her and brought her across his lap, holding her securely against his chest. She was shivering, but he knew it wasn't from the cool early-morning air. What she had finally admitted was a shock and nothing he could say would help her right now. He would let his strength speak for him.

Michele closed her eyes as his fingers gently caressed her neck and shoulders. His warmth seeped into her, soothing her. She had admitted to him what she hadn't been able to admit to herself. Amazingly enough, he hadn't been repulsed by what she'd said.

Raising her lashes, she met his gaze. "How did you know?"

"About your love-hate feelings for your mother?"

She nodded.

"I've been there. Even after my mother abandoned me, I made excuses for her to anyone who asked about her, especially to myself. It wasn't until I got into one fight too many with a kid much bigger than I was who said something derogatory about my mother that Rocky sat me down and made me admit I was angry with her, not with the kid who had beat the stuffings out of me. He made me realize I hated her for thinking so little of me that she could simply walk away and never look back. She made me feel insignificant, and I hated her for that."

"I wish I'd known Rocky. He sounds very special."

"He was a cantankerous old goat, but I would probably be dead if it wasn't for him."

"For someone who keeps saying he doesn't get involved with anyone, you were certainly involved with him. And there's Sutherland and his children. You are practically a member of their family. I wouldn't call that being uninvolved."

The pressure of his hands on her back changed, his fingers enticing instead of soothing. "I'd rather work on my involvement with you."

"Work? Are you sure that's the word you want to use?" she teased. "I'm not sure I like you thinking it's hard work to be in bed with me."

In one smooth action, he tumbled her onto her back and moved to lay between her legs. He made sure she could feel just how hard his involvement with her was.

Chapter Twelve

Michele parked her car behind the clinic on Monday morning and adjusted the pair of sunglasses she'd put on as she was leaving her cottage. The sun had been up for barely an hour in a cloudless sky, and the glasses were necessary to shield her tired eyes from the bright light.

The way they felt at the moment, a two-watt bulb would be too much.

Bud would no doubt question her about her lack of sleep when he saw her bleary eyes. His naturally snoopy nature wouldn't be able to resist. She was glad she had the puppies to use an an excuse. She certainly wasn't about to tell him how she had occupied last night. Or with whom.

She smiled to herself as she shut off the engine. The last couple of nights weren't the only times her sleep had been interrupted for special feedings, but Sunday night was the first time she'd had company.

Seeing Cord sitting on the floor tickling the tummy of a delighted puppy was a picture she would carry in her memory for a very long time. Probably the rest of her life. His dark hair had been mussed, his wrinkled shirt opened down the front. His jawline had been rough with the shadow of a beard, and his feet had been bare beneath the denim jeans he'd tugged on when they'd heard the puppies whining and yipping for attention.

After she gave them their medicine, she'd shown Cord how to dip his finger into the warm fortified milk and offer it to a puppy to lick. With each dip of his finger, he was to move his hand closer to the source of the milk until the puppy realized he would get more faster if he drank from the saucer. Three of them had caught on but two were slower in figuring it out. Michele worked with one and Cord the other. If they couldn't get them to the saucer, they would have to feed the two puppies with a bottle.

Cord chose the runt of the litter and worked with him with extreme patience, finally persuading the puppy to approach the saucer of milk. Unfortunately, the eager student thought his whole body should be in the saucer, too.

Michele looked up when she heard Cord chuckle and saw him reach out to retrieve the puppy from his headfirst plunge into the milk. When his protégé finally began lapping in earnest, Cord smiled like a proud father whose son had just kicked the winning field goal.

It had been an odd moment for Michele to realize she was in love with him.

There was no other explanation for the glow of happiness welling up deep inside her whenever she looked at him, thought of him, touched him, she reflected as she opened her car door. Just because she'd never felt like this before didn't mean she couldn't identify the emotion.

She loved Cord Thomas.

Which had made it even harder to say goodbye when it was time for him to leave that morning. She'd better adjust to seeing Cord drive away, she reminded herself. Having an affair with him was going to mean a number of farewells when they returned to their separate lives.

Nothing had been said about the future other than Cord promising to call her. Then he'd kissed her long and deeply before driving away.

If time could be preserved in some way, Michele would have chosen Sunday night and early Monday morning. In between feeding the puppies, the hours were filled with ordinary activities that somehow became extraordinary.

A shower had turned into a sensual adventure that lasted until the hot water ran out. Preparing breakfast had been a chancy operation with playful puppies underfoot and Cord rearranging the food items in her refrigerator, which made it difficult for her to find anything. But it was neat.

As the sun came up, they had walked hand in hand on the beach, occasionally picking up shells as they lazily shared bits and pieces of their lives with each other.

After they returned to the cottage, Michelle checked on the sleeping puppies. When she left the kitchen, she found Cord going through her selection of cassettes and CDs. She watched as he chose a tape and put it in the player, his movements economical and oddly graceful as he closed the case and pushed the correct buttons.

He turned as slow sensuous saxophones played in the background and he looked directly into her eyes. He lifted a hand out to her, and she stepped forward to take it. Cord drew her into his arms and held her securely against his body for a long moment, simply holding her as the music swirled around them. Then he began to sway back and forth in time to the music, eventually leading her into a sensual dance that went on and on.

Losing sleep had been a small price to pay for hours of passionate urgency, swamping need and a devastating closeness she savored like a priceless gift.

She wasn't looking forward to returning to her cottage tonight after work. She'd dropped the puppies off at Opal's house on her way to the clinic after Cord had left. She would still have her dogs and cats for company, but Cord's absence would leave a large empty hole in her life that memories could never fill.

Sighing deeply, she opened her car door. She had hoped to have a little time to herself that morning in the clinic, but she wasn't the only one who had arrived early, she noticed as she looked around the parking lot. Bud's pride and joy, his classic Thunderbird, was in its usual place. However, the custom-made cover he usually put over the car to protect the paint from the gritty sand was missing, which meant he'd been in a hurry. It was his weekend to be on call and obviously an emergency had brought him to the clinic Sunday night or early Monday morning.

The sound of a woman crying was the first ominous thing Michele heard when she let herself in the back door. As she rushed down the hall, she recognized the voice of the man who was trying to comfort the weeping woman. The man was Bruce Denham.

Fear clutched Michele's stomach with sharp claws. Something had happened to Willoughby again. Michele had seen a few other animals with a penchant for swallowing all sorts of odd objects, but Willoughby was too small to get away with ingesting anything other than dog food. Quickening her steps, Michele dropped her case on the first laboratory counter she passed, removed her sunglasses and hurried toward the surgery room. Her exhaustion had been replaced by a sense of urgency.

An hour later, she ruthlessly tore off her surgical gloves and threw them in the closest receptacle. She had to be content to take her anger and frustration out on the gloves. Everyone else was feeling as badly as she was.

Especially Bud. He'd done everything humanly possible to save the little dog, but she knew he was beating himself up inside wondering if there was something he'd missed, some procedure he had neglected to do. She went through the same soul-searching and self-recriminations herself whenever she failed to save an animal.

There was nothing she could say that would make him feel any better, so she placed her hand on his shoulder briefly in silent understanding.

"Do you want me to talk to Bruce and his wife?" she asked quietly.

Bud shook his head slowly. "I'll do it. Thanks anyway." He'd been staring at his hands. Now he looked up at Michele. "Maybe if I'd gotten to him sooner, I could have stopped the internal bleeding."

"Don't do this to yourself, Bud. We save a lot of animals, but occasionally, we lose one no matter what we do."

His sigh came from deep within him. "My head knows that. It's my heart that's giving me problems."

Michele squeezed his shoulder, then went out of the surgery. The staff had arrived at their usual time and were going about their work with a subdued silence. No matter how experienced they were, everyone felt the loss of an animal as though it was the first one.

Dixie was standing in front of the open refrigerator door, gazing at the assortment of medications, unable to see what she was looking for through the tears filling her eyes. Michele walked up to her and put her arm around the girl's waist, shutting the door with her free hand.

"Take ten minutes in the lunchroom if you want, Dixie." Experience had taught Michele that taking care of other animals helped soothe the bruise on the heart left by losing one. "Then I'll need your help with Bowser. He's scheduled for his shots this morning, and you know how fond he is of the needle."

Dixie gave her a watery smile. "I'll be okay. It was just that Willoughby was so special."

"I know." Michele worked past the lump of sadness in her throat. "They all are."

Gail called out to her that she was wanted on the phone.

Raising her voice so Gail could hear her, Michele said, "Take a message and tell them I'll call them back if it isn't an emergency."

"I think you might want to take this one."

Michele closed her eyes for a moment. When Gail used that particular cautious tone of voice, it usually meant the phone call was private, personal and usually had something to do with Michele's mother.

Expecting Mrs. Walcott or a policeman on the line, when she took the call in her office, she was surprised when she heard Cord's voice. Since he'd left only a little over an hour ago, he couldn't possibly be in Virginia Beach yet.

All she'd said was hello and Cord somehow detected something in her voice that made him ask immediately, "What's wrong?"

She could hear unusual sounds on the line, and she realized he was on his car phone. "Why are you calling me from your car? Were you in an accident? Where are you?"

"I crossed the state line about twenty minutes ago. You don't sound right. Did something happen with your mother?"

"Not that I know of." She wasn't going to make him drag it out of her. Even though she'd never had anyone to talk to in the past but her friend Barbara, Michele found it remarkably easy to confide in Cord. "Do you remember the Yorkshire terrier who ran between your legs the first time you came to the clinic?"

"I'd find it easier to forget my own name. What about him?"

"Willoughby swallowed a nail sometime during the night. By the time his owner discovered something was wrong and called Bud, who was taking emergencies, it was too late. The nail had done too much damage internally."

"Damn," he muttered. "I'm sorry, babe. He was a scrappy little guy."

Swallowing with difficulty, she cleared her throat. "Yes, he was." Oddly enough, she felt better after sharing her pain with Cord. "Why are you calling so soon after you left? Did you forget something?"

There were a few seconds of dead air on the line. Then he said, "This is a bad time to ask this, but would it be possible for you to take today and possibly tomorrow off and come to Virginia Beach again?"

It wasn't so much what he said as the tone of his voice. It wasn't a casual question, so she gave him an honest answer. "It would mean rearranging appointments and getting Bud to take the ones that can't be canceled, but I can if it's important."

"It is," he said soberly. "I just called the house to tell Michael I'd be dropping by to see him this morning, and the housekeeper told me he was taken to the hospital during the night. Hannah tried to call me on the boat and on my mobile phone around two in the morning before they left for the hospital."

"They didn't know you were with me," she guessed.

Even though she hadn't phrased her comment as a question, he answered it anyway. "I left my pager number with Michael, but he was in no condition to give it to Hannah."

"Hannah and Neal must be so frightened."

"They rode in the ambulance with Michael. I imagine they're still there. I'm on my way to the hospital now."

"It's Michael's heart again, isn't it?"

"I don't know," he said hesitantly. "I suppose so. The housekeeper said he was having chest pains."

"My visit upset him, didn't it?" She began pacing the floor, which wasn't easy in the confined space of her office. "I knew I shouldn't have gone to see him.

I told you it wasn't a good idea. The only thing my visit accomplished was to cause him to have another heart attack.''

"We don't know that." For a few seconds, there was only the sound of static on the line. Then Cord said, "You're his daughter, Michele. You should be there."

"Hannah and Neal have enough to contend with without having a stranger being thrust on them."

"I'm not going to argue with you, Michele," he said roughly. "The kids need you, and damn it, so do I. He means a lot to me, too."

"Cord, I—"

He didn't allow her to give him any more excuses. "You either stay a stranger to him or you accept the fact you have a father who might be dying, and get your tail to the hospital to see him before it's too late. He's at Virginia Beach General Hospital in intensive care. That's where I'll be with your brother and your sister."

Michele heard a click on the line, then nothing. Cord had disconnected the call. She replaced the receiver and sank down on her chair. Resting her elbows on the desk, she held her head in her hands. The calico cat, who had been watching her from the top of the nearest bookcase, jumped the small distance to the desk. Boots sidled up to Michele's bent head and rubbed against her hair, his deep rolling purr the only sound in the room.

Michele lifted her head and automatically stroked the cat's thick fur.

"What do you think I should do, Boots? I have two choices. Either I stay here and continue as I have before or go to the hospital and possibly change my life forever."

The cat sat directly in front of her and stared into Michele's eyes with unflinching calm.

Michele reached out to scratch the cat's ear, smiling slightly when Boots closed his eyes in pure ecstasy. When Michele ceased the caressing motion, the cat nudged her fingers as a hint for her to continue the stroking.

"That's it, Boots," she murmured. "Don't be shy about what you want. Scratch and claw and make noise if you want something."

Suddenly she got to her feet. Looking down at the cat, she said, "You might have the right idea on how to handle things after all."

Michele stepped around the desk and started walking toward the door.

"Bud?" she yelled, scaring Boots so badly, he hunched his back like a Halloween cat and hissed.

Her partner answered from examination room 2. "I'm in here."

She hurried to the doorway and asked, "Is your brother-in-law down from D.C. this week?"

"Yeah. Why?"

"Tell him he can have free medical care for his two Shih Tzus if he'll fly me to Norfolk Airport as soon as possible," she said quickly, naming the closest airport to Virginia Beach.

Bud was about to put a stain strip to a dog's eye. "Okay. I'll call him as soon as I finish here." As he worked, he commented, "He has to keep his plane in Manteo, but he can touch down at Kill Devil Hills, which will be closer for you to get to."

"Whatever, as long as it's soon. And I'll need you to fill in again for me. It's an emergency, otherwise I wouldn't ask."

"No problem. I hope it's nothing too serious."

Michele bit her lip as she thought about Michael Sutherland's pale face. "I do, too." It was then that she made an astonishing announcement, although Bud couldn't possibly realize just how amazing it was.

"My father's been taken to the hospital."

An hour later, she followed the directions given to her at the information desk to the intensive-care unit. The elevator doors whisked open, and Michele stepped out. The waiting room was relatively small, or perhaps only seemed small due to the number of people filling the chairs and standing around. Cord was pacing back and forth in front of chairs occupied with solemn people either leafing listlessly through magazines, staring at the floor or talking quietly to each other.

Hannah and the young man sitting next to her followed each step Cord took, their eyes wide and frightened, as though he were the only anchor they had to cling to in a stormy sea. He probably was, she thought, her heart going out to them. Michele wondered if their mother had been notified about Michael's condition and would be coming to be with her children. Hannah had said they had a close relationship with her even though they lived with their father.

When Cord turned to continue his pacing, he glanced up and saw Michele. With a determined stride, he closed the distance between them and reached for her. He pulled her into his arms, burying his face in the soft curve of her neck. He held her so tightly, she could barely breathe.

The urgency in his hold made her even more tense than she'd been when she arrived.

Lifting his head, he said quietly, "I'm glad you came."

"How is he?"

"He's holding on." He glanced at the large wall clock between the elevators. "How did you get here so quickly? I wasn't expecting you for another hour."

"You were so sure I was coming?"

He grinned. "Oh, yeah. I was sure. I know you better than you know yourself. When it came down to the wire, you couldn't help doing the right thing."

"I'm glad you were so sure. I almost didn't get on the plane."

"Plane?"

"Bud's brother-in-law commutes between Washington, D.C., and the Outer Banks by flying his own Beechcraft. There's a small airfield near the Wright Brothers' Monument in Kill Devil Hills, and luckily Paul was planning a trip to D.C. this morning and agreed to fly into Norfolk and drop me off." She touched the side of his face. "You look exhausted. What can I do to help?"

He brought his hand up to cover hers. "You've already helped more than you know by coming when I needed you."

"Have you seen Michael?"

"About an hour ago. We're only allowed to see him for ten minutes every two hours, so we have to rely on whatever the nurses feel like telling us in between." He took her hand. "Come and say hi to the kids."

Michele was relieved to see a faint smile of welcome on Hannah's strained face. Neal didn't even glance her way until Hannah nudged him in the side to get his attention. When he scowled at her, Hannah jerked her head toward Cord and Michele. Having never met Michele before, the boy looked from her to Cord, then back again without much interest. He stood politely when Michele and Cord approached them.

"Neal, this is Michele LaBrock."

The boy was clearly puzzled why she was there, but remembered his manners enough to extend his right hand and murmur, "Nice to meet you."

"Hello, Neal," she replied as she shook his hand. Turning to Hannah, she said, "I thought about what you said about being outnumbered by all these males. I came to even the odds a little."

"Thank you." To her brother, she said, "She's the one I told you about who is a veterinarian and takes care of animals."

"That's what vets do," he pointed out with the customary superiority of an older sibling. His gaze dropped to Michele's hand in Cord's tight grip. "I guess you know Cord. That's why you're here."

"I know your father, too. I could use a cup of coffee. Have you two had any breakfast?"

Both youngsters shook their heads and looked at Cord, who nodded his agreement. "I should have thought of that myself. You two go with Michele to the cafeteria and get something to eat."

It was Neal who voiced their concern. "But what about Dad? What if...?"

"I'll be right here. If anything happens, I'll send word for you if it's necessary. You heard your dad's doctor. He said it will be a while before they know for sure if Michael is out of danger.''

Hannah went willingly enough, but Neal was obviously reluctant to leave the waiting room. Hannah made up for Neal's sullen silence by describing the trip to the hospital in the back of the ambulance with the siren blaring away. The girl kept trying to include Neal in the conversation, but she received only an occasional grunt for her trouble.

Michele was amused to see that the boy managed to speak up easily enough when it was his turn to order what he wanted to eat. She noticed his lack of sleep didn't appear to interfere with his appetite.

Without staring at him outright, Michele surreptitiously studied Neal. He resembled his sister more than he did his father, with the same brown hair and brown eyes. He was a head taller than Hannah and awkwardly thin as though his height was waiting for his weight to catch up, and his muscles didn't know what the heck was going on. Neal was more reserved than his younger sister, although Michele thought that could be because of his father's illness.

Neal waited until they were seated at a small table in the corner of the cafeteria before he asked the question Michele had been expecting.

''Why are you here, Miss LaBrock?''

''Neal,'' his sister said in disgust. ''That's rude.''

Michele appreciated Hannah's defense, but it was a fair question. During the flight to Virginia Beach, she'd given a lot of thought to her answer, knowing the subject was bound to come up.

''You've gone to a lot of trouble to come here,'' he continued when she didn't immediately answer. ''I've never seen you before, and you are apparently involved with Cord and not dating my dad. So, are you some kind of general do-gooder, or just trying to make points with Cord?''

Michele was impressed with his ability to aim right for the target rather than take some polite practice shots.

''It isn't necessary to go into the details now, except to say there's a family connection between your family and mine. That's basically why I'm here.''

''You mean we're related?'' he asked after nearly choking on a french fry.

''That's what I mean.'' She hoped they would accept that explanation without wanting to know the facts behind them. Hannah might have let it go at that. Michele wasn't so sure Neal would.

''How come we've never met you before?'' he asked suspiciously.

''The relationship was only recently researched by your father. He sent Cord to Nags Head, North Carolina, where I live, to tell me what he'd found out about our family connection.''

''Did you know Cord before then?''

Michele had a feeling she knew which direction Neal was heading, but she couldn't think of a single detour to take to get out of his way.

''No, I didn't.''

Hannah asked, ''Is that why you came to see Daddy with Uncle Cord the other day? Because you're part of the family?''

She nodded. ''That's why Cord phoned me this morning to tell me your father had been taken to the hospital. He knew I would want to know.''

''But Uncle Cord said he was with you last night. That's why we couldn't reach him when we tried to call him early this morning. Ouch!'' she exclaimed when Neal kicked her under the table. "What did you do that for?''

"'Cause you were butting into something that's none of your business, that's why. Remember Dad told us to stay out of Cord's love life?''

The last sentence was said in almost a whisper but loud enough for Michele to hear. She wondered if Neal meant for her to overhear his comment.

Hannah gave Michele a shy smile. "I'm sorry, Michele. I was just curious why you would say Uncle Cord phoned you if he was with you.''

"He was in his car on his way back to Virginia Beach when he called your house to talk to your father this morning. That's when he learned your father was in the hospital. I came as soon as I could in case there was something I could do to help.''

"Like buying us a hamburger? How is that going to help Dad?''

"Not much, I admit, but it might make you feel better if you have something to eat.'' She smiled. "Who knows, a hamburger or two might even improve your attitude.''

"Sorry.'' Color deepened the color on his cheeks. "Hannah's right. I've been rude.''

"Don't worry about it. You're concerned about your father so I'm making allowances. If it helps you to blow off a little steam in my direction, go ahead.''

"Nah, that's okay.'' He picked up several french fries and dipped then into a generous puddle of catsup. "You were right. I was hungry.''

"I probably should have suggested eggs and bacon or oatmeal for breakfast instead of letting you order a hamburger and french fries. They would be better for you." She saw the faces they made and chuckled. "I won't tell if you don't."

Hannah was more tactful than her brother but just as curious. "Are we supposed to call you Aunt Michele or cousin or something like that? You haven't said how we're related."

"Michele will do just fine," she answered. She pushed back her chair. "While you two finish your hamburgers, I'm going to order some coffee to take to Cord. He could probably use a cup about now."

Whether it was the break away from the solemn waiting room or the effects of the food, both Neal and Hannah were in better spirits by the time they rejoined Cord in the waiting room.

Their mood improved even more an hour later when Michael's doctor came out to tell them that their father had turned the corner and would recover. They were still going to keep him in intensive care for a while, but only as a precaution. The doctor smiled at Neal's and Hannah's grinning, relieved faces and told them they could go in to see their father for a few minutes, and then Michael would need to rest.

Cord walked with the children toward the door of the intensive-care unit. Michele suddenly felt light-headed with relief and sank down on one of the chairs. The strength of her feelings for the man she'd met only once was staggering. Evidently, blood was thicker than water, she mused.

She thought Cord had gone in with Hannah and Neal, so when he placed his hand on her shoulder, she nearly jumped out of her skin.

Glancing up, she said, "I thought you were with the kids."

"Family only," he murmured as he sat down beside her. "You could have gone in with them, you know."

She shook her head. "They should see him alone. In the cafeteria, they were trying to figure out where I fit in. I explained to them that only recently was it discovered that I'm related to the Sutherland family. Neal didn't accept me automatically the way Hannah did the other day. I had to tell him something."

"You can't put it off indefinitely," he warned. "They're going to need to know sometime. Michael will see to that."

"Let's leave things the way they are for now."

"And what way are they, Michele?" he asked roughly. "Are you going to tell me this weekend didn't change anything between us?"

"I'm getting real tired of explaining myself." She leaned closer to try to keep their conversation from reaching the other people in the waiting room. In a low voice, she said, "Last night changed everything. Nothing will ever be the same, and it's all your fault. You had no more than backed out of my driveway and the puppies started yelping. The little one you fed early this morning wouldn't have anything to do with me and kept scurrying around the kitchen looking for you. When I was getting dressed, I couldn't see what I was doing because I was crying, and I put on one red sock and a yellow one with purple stripes." She pulled up her pant legs to show him she was still wearing them. "I didn't notice until I was on the plane."

His voice was gentle, his touch tender as he cupped her face. "Why were you crying?"

"Because I didn't want you to leave, you big dummy." When he smiled, she wanted to hit him. "It's not funny."

"I'm not smiling because I'm laughing at you. There are other reasons people smile, like when they're happy."

"Well, if my crying makes you happy, you're going to be hysterical the next time you leave, because I doubt if I'll take that goodbye any better."

Cord would have chosen a better place to have this discussion than a crowded waiting room with the faint smell of antiseptic in the air. A declaration like that deserved more from him than holding her hand, which was all he was allowing himself at the moment.

As he looked at her, he wondered if she realized what she had admitted.

He should be wondering why he wasn't feeling alarmed at the thought of her being more serious about their relationship than he had counted on. Knowing she had cried when he left had filled him with a warm glow that she cared that much, not irritation or panic or dread as he'd felt before when a woman started getting emotional or possessive or clingy.

There, in the waiting room of the hospital, surrounded by strangers, Cord finally understood why he was holding tightly to her hand instead of flinging it aside and running for dear life.

He was in love with her.

It was the only explanation for the way he felt. He'd known his desire for her was different the first time he'd felt her close around him when they'd made love. How different he hadn't had time to analyze. Now he

knew why he had felt such overwhelming joy and ful-
fillment when he'd become part of her.

He was unaware of the stark shock in his gaze when
he looked at her. The realization was too much to take
in at once. Dropping her hand, he stood and walked
over to the drinking fountain without any explanation to her. If he hadn't put some distance between
them, he might have done something incredibly idi-
otic like get down on bended knee and swear his undying love to her in front of all the people in the
waiting room.

After he had taken as much time as he dared, he
turned back to where Michele sat. One glance at her
face showed him the harm he had done by abruptly
walking away from her at that particular moment
without an explanation. She had misinterpreted his
actions, thinking he had rejected her admission that
she cared about him.

She had completely closed herself off from him
again, and he nearly groaned aloud in frustration.

He started toward her, but before he could reach
her, Pilar Sutherland, Michael's ex-wife and Hannah
and Neal's mother, entered the waiting room. Looking every inch the successful business executive she
was, Pilar glanced around the room.

Her rust-colored suit and yellow blouse went well
with her dark brown hair and eyes, which was the
general idea behind her choice. Pilar Vega Sutherland
left nothing to chance. She calculated, computed and
analyzed every hypothesis at least once, sometimes
twice—three times if necessary. These traits made her
supremely qualified as the president of a chain of
Victoriana gift shops, but not as a wife.

She spotted Cord, and a look of relief briefly replaced her worried expression.

A muscle clenched in Cord's jaw as he changed course to meet her. "Thanks for coming, Pilar," he said as he leaned over to kiss her cheek.

"I appreciate your calling me about Michael. How is he?"

"The doctor just told us that he's going to make it."

Tears filled the woman's eyes and she threw herself into Cord's arms. "Thank God!" Stepping back, she asked, "How are the children?"

"Better now that they know he'll be all right. They went in to see him for a few minutes." He took her arm. "There's someone I want you to meet."

"Really?" The woman's gaze followed his as they walked toward where Michele was sitting. "Don't tell me you've finally decided to throw away the little black book, Cord." She stopped suddenly and stared at Michele.

"My God," she said softly.

"Pilar? What is it?" asked Cord with concern. "Are you feeling sick?"

"It's her, isn't it?" she asked Cord even though Michele was only three feet away. "It's Michael's oldest daughter."

Michele and Cord were both stunned speechless by her announcement and stared at her with almost identical expressions of disbelief.

Cord recovered first. "How did you know that?"

Instead of answering him, Pilar walked up to Michele and held out her hand. "I'm so pleased to finally meet you. Michael must be over the moon to see you after so many years."

"I don't understand," murmured Michele as she stood and stared at Pilar.

"I haven't introduced myself, and Cord has apparently forgotten what few manners he has. I'm Pilar Sutherland, Michael's second wife. Or I should say his second ex-wife."

Michele automatically extended her hand to clasp the other woman's briefly.

"I didn't think anyone but Michael and Cord knew about me."

"Before we were married, Michael told me all about you and showed me pictures he had gotten from your school every year." She inclined her head to examine Michele more closely. "You resemble your pictures enough—you couldn't have been anyone else."

Michele looked at Cord. "Did you know he had my school pictures?"

Shaking his head, he answered, "He told me he lost track of you when you graduated from high school. Evidently that was the last contact he had."

Pilar adjusted the shoulder strap of her purse, her smile one of genuine pleasure. "I bet the children are tickled pink to have an older sister. This is so exciting."

Before either Michele or Cord could warn her not to say anything to Neal or Hannah, the teenagers burst out of the intensive-care unit, grinning from ear to ear. When they saw their mother, they rushed forward, their young faces reflecting their joy and relief.

Michele stepped out of the way to give the teenagers room to hug their mother.

Their excitement was contagious as they told their mother that Michael was going to be fine. He'd just promised them that he'd be home as soon as he could. He still had all those nasty tubes and things attached to beeping, blinking machines. But he had smiled and reassured them that he would be okay.

"That is wonderful news, darlings. How brave you've been through all this. I'm very proud of both of you. Do you want to come and stay with me until your father can come home? I have a couple of buying trips coming up, but I could cancel them if you want to be with me."

Hannah glanced at Neal, who spoke for both of them. Hesitating briefly, Neal explained, "With school and everything, it would be easier if we stayed home. Cord can stay like last time." A look of minor irritation crossed his young features as he added, "I don't need a baby-sitter, you know. I'm seventeen, for crying out loud."

In a soothing voice used by every mother on earth at one time or other, Pilar consoled her son. "We all know you don't require supervision, Neal. But looking after Hannah wouldn't allow you much time for all those sports activities you are involved in. With Cord overseeing the care and feeding of your sister, you will have more freedom."

Grumbling, Neal said, "He stands over us to make sure we do our homework."

"A truly despicable act of cruelty, I'm sure," his mother said dryly. She looked in Michele's direction. "Perhaps your sister could stay with you, too."

Michele closed her eyes briefly to absorb the impact of Pilar's statement. When she eventually opened them, everyone was looking at her. Hannah's face had

become pale with shock. Neal's was flushed with fury.
Pilar was smiling.

And Cord resembled someone who had just swallowed a bug.

Chapter Thirteen

After a full minute of silence during which everyone simply stared at Michele, they looked at one another and suddenly all began to talk at once, the result being that no one could possibly hear what anyone else was saying.

Except Michele, who didn't say a word.

She heard Neal mutter a mild expletive, which resulted in his mother automatically scolding him for swearing.

Hannah kept saying, "Sister? She's my sister?" over and over.

Cord told Pilar that the boy's response was perfectly reasonable under the circumstances. Then he tried to answer Hannah's question by repeating the answer several times. "Yes, Hannah. Michele is your sister."

Pilar apologized to everyone in general for speaking out of turn. She had assumed Hannah and Neal knew about Michele.

Neal wanted to know why his dad hadn't told them about Michele before. "Hannah and I had a right to know we had a sister, damn it."

Pilar said disgustedly, "You swear again, young man, and I'll wash your mouth out with soap."

Hannah's eyes gleamed with anticipation.

"Damn it, Pilar," Cord said impatiently. "Will you stop harping on the kid?"

She turned on him. "Now I know where he learns such profanity. Perhaps if you cleaned up your language when you're around the children, they wouldn't pick up curse words."

Cord's reply was another irreverent word that brought color to Pilar's cheeks and a devilish amusement to Neal's eyes. "Could we get back to the original subject instead of criticizing Neal's choice of language?" he snapped. "Which I think fit the situation perfectly, by the way."

Since her presence was the cause of the commotion, Michele was overwhelmed with guilt. Her presence had disrupted their close family ties at a time when they needed one another and had enough on their minds with worrying about Michael's health. Somehow she had to make them understand her relationship to the family didn't change anything between them.

She stepped into the middle of the fracas. Literally.

"Stop it!" she demanded in a low voice, which they all heard, even though they were all responding to Cord's comments at the time. "I can't stand hearing all of you fight when I know I'm the cause of it. Right now Michael's health is what's important. Whether or not I'm related to Michael shouldn't make any difference in your relationship to each other or to him. You all have survived up until now just fine without knowing who I was. Let's leave it that way. I suggest you all go back to Michael's house and make plans for having him home again."

Cord frowned. "You make it sound as though you don't plan on coming with us."

"You can explain the situation to Neal and Hannah much better than I could. After all, you started the whole thing by coming to Nags Head to find me. Well, you found me," she said shakily. "And look what happened. Michael is in intensive care and you are all fighting. It's not worth it, Cord. I'm not going to be the cause of this family breaking up."

"The family isn't breaking up," he said with a puzzled frown. "We're just arguing, that's all. It happens in the best of families. Michael is not in the hospital because of the stress of meeting you, Michele," he added hastily. "The doctor explained that it was a reaction to one of the medications he was given when he got out of the hospital the first time. It had nothing to do with you. You're right about one thing. We need to get out of here so we can explain to the kids what happened in the past that led to your being here today."

Michele didn't agree or disagree with him. It was as though she hadn't hard a word he said. She met Hannah's confused eyes, then Neal's wary gaze. "I didn't want either of you upset or hurt. I'm sorry you had to find out this way, but nothing has changed in your family."

"How can you say that?" argued Neal. "We've had a sister somewhere who pops up out of nowhere, and you say nothing has changed?"

Including Neal with a glance, Michele tried to explain. "You two are still the most important people in your father's life. That hasn't changed. I was a part of his life a long time ago, almost in another lifetime. When he became seriously ill, he wanted to see me. Cord came to Nags Head and asked me to visit your father, so I did. I never meant to upset either of you by coming here."

With the deadly aim of the genuinely innocent, Hannah asked, "Why do you keep calling him our father when he's your father, too?"

"He's a stranger to me in the same way I'm a stranger to you."

"Your mother was married to Daddy?"

"Yes. They were divorced when I was two years old."

Pilar stopped Hannah from asking another question. "That's enough for now."

"But..."

"No buts and no more questions." Turning to Michele, Pilar said, "I'm terribly sorry I've put you on the spot like this. I took it for granted that Michael had told the children about you."

Michele shook her head. "It's not your fault." She looked at Cord briefly before returning her gaze to Pilar. "If anyone's to blame for this, it's me. I should have followed my first instincts and stayed away." She lifted a hand to touch the side of Hannah's face. "I'll never regret meeting you. Take care of your father and each other, okay?"

She started to walk away, but she had only taken two steps when Cord caught up with her and gripped her arm.

"You don't get out of the family that easily, sweetheart," he murmured as he drew her with him toward the elevator.

He was closely followed by the others, who had suddenly run out of arguments. Rather than try to talk in the elevator or in the corridors, Michele waited until they were outside the entrance before she tried to leave them again.

"I know how relieved you are that Michael is going to be all right," she said to no one in particular. "I'd like to call in a couple of days to check on his progress if that's okay."

Cord had to have heard her since he was standing close to her side, but he acted as though he hadn't heard a word she said.

"Pilar, can the kids ride with you to Michael's?" he asked. "I'll take Michele with me, and we'll meet you there."

The older woman nodded and turned to walk in the direction of one of the parking lots. Hannah and Neal followed, with Neal trying to persuade his mother to let him drive. "I have my driving permit now. Dad lets me drive his car sometimes."

Pilar's voice carried back to Cord and Michele. "Well, you aren't driving my car, so just forget it."

Cord's hold on Michele's arm tightened enough to make her aware that he was determined she was going with him. "Cord, I don't want to go back to Michael's. I can call a taxi to take me to the airport, and you can return to his place or to the marina or wherever you were going to go after you knew Michael would be all right.''

''You might as well accept the fact you're coming with me, Michele. Then we can eliminate that argument and move on to the next one. Like why you're shutting the kids out instead of letting them get to know you.''

Walking along beside him, she kept her gaze on the asphalt. ''When Michael comes home from the hospital, he'll need peace and quiet, not have his children upset with him because he didn't tell them about me. They have a close relationship with their father. I don't want to jeopardize that.''

''You haven't hurt their relationship with Michael.''

''How can you say that? You heard them arguing. You even joined in. Can you imagine what it will do to Michael when he learns his children are alienated from him because of me?''

He stopped near his car and placed his hands on her shoulders to hold her in front of him. ''Michele, they were only arguing. They do that a lot. I've been around them during the last ten years, and believe me, they bicker like that all the time. Neal and his mother also crash heads once in a while. It's part of being a teenager and the parent of a teenager. It goes with the territory.'' He brought his hands up to cup her face. ''All families disagree at one time or another. It's not the end of the world, only one of the louder parts of family life.''

Her eyes went wide with surprise. ''You mean that fighting like that is normal?''

Cord realized she was serious. Then it occurred to him that her overreaction was due to the lack of a family life to compare with the Sutherlands'. She had been haphazardly raised an only child by an alcoholic mother. It wasn't surprising that Michele thought the words exchanged by Hannah and Neal would have torn up the family relationship.

"Not only is it normal," he explained patiently. "It's almost mandatory." He unlocked the door and held it open for her. "We'll go back to Michael's, and you can see for yourself that no harm has been done to Hannah and Neal's relationship with each other or with their father."

Michele slid onto the seat but didn't say a word. A minute or so later, he joined her and started the engine.

As he drove to Michael's house, Cord didn't try to initiate any conversation to fill the silence in the car. Several times, he glanced over at her, but Michele continued to look out the window.

He would bet his new six-hundred-dollar fishing reel that Michele wasn't enjoying the scenery she was supposedly seeing. Her penchant for keeping her feelings locked up tight inside was going to have to be eliminated somehow. He didn't play games with himself; nor did he plan on playing them with her. That left the truth, but he knew she wasn't ready to hear that yet.

She might never be ready, he thought grimly.

Hannah and Neal were waiting in the driveway when Cord drove up. Hannah waved, and Neal stood straight and tall beside her, his sharp gaze never leaving the car until Cord parked it out front. Then Neal walked around to Michele's side of the car and opened the door for her as though he'd been doing it all his life.

She looked up at him as he stood near the door, a guarded wariness in her eyes.

He looked a trifle sheepish. "Dad told me that I'm supposed to open doors for ladies even though some girls don't want guys to do that much anymore."

"Thank you," she said quietly as she got out of the car. "Your father is right. Most women do like such polite gestures. I do, anyway."

When Michele was standing next to him, he shut the door but didn't move toward the house. He looked at the car, in Cord's direction, then finally at his feet.

Michele got the impression he wanted to say something. "What is it, Neal?"

"Ah," he murmured as he lifted his head, "it's really true, then, about you being our sister?"

"Half sister. Yes, it's true. Your father was married to my mother a long time ago."

"That explains why you're so old."

Michele bit the inside of her lip to keep from smiling. "I guess it does."

"Well, I was thinking on the way home." An eagerness entered his voice that made Michele a little nervous. "Dad always said that family is supposed to stick together, you know? We're to help each other and look out for one another."

He paused as though expecting her to say something, but she hadn't the faintest idea why he wanted to make those points. "Do you?" she finally asked.

"Huh?"

"Do you look out for Hannah?"

He shrugged. "Sometimes. When she isn't being a pain in the . . . Never mind. What I mean is, if a member of the family asks a favor of another, we're supposed to try to do what we can to help."

"I see," she murmured, although so far, the reason for the conversation was still a mystery. "Is there some favor you wanted to ask me to do for you?"

"I don't know. It depends."

"On what?"

"On what kind of car you drive," he said in a rush. "I was hoping you have a neat sports car or something like that. Being a vet and all, I figured you might have a Corvette or a Porsche. Maybe I could borrow it sometime after I get my license."

Feeling as though she was letting him down somehow, she said, "I have a small station wagon."

He tried bravely to hide his disappointment, but it came through when he said, "Oh."

Cord had heard Neal's less-than-subtle hint and came around the car to put his hand at Michele's waist to direct her toward the front door. "Along with instructions on helping out family members, Michael also taught you to invite people into the house rather than make them stand in the driveway."

Falling into step beside Cord, Neal said, "Dad never said that."

"Well, he should have." Walking beside Michele up the steps, he asked Neal, "How's the driving coming?"

"Not too good. How can I get the experience everyone says I need if no one lets me drive?"

Neal gave Cord a hopeful glance, which changed to disappointment when Cord drawled, "Good question. Let me know when you find another sucker who'll let you drive his car."

"Jeez," Neal said disgustedly. "I told you I didn't see that cement mixer pull out of the neighbor's driveway that time you took me out. And I missed it, didn't I?''

"If the fender of my car had another coat of paint on it, you wouldn't have missed it. That's how close you came." Remembering how he used to nag Rocky to let him drive, he relented enough to say, "If you come right home from school one day next week, I'll take you to the elementary school parking lot up the street. There won't be anything for you to run into, and you'll get some driving time. How's that?''

Cord's reward was a high five and a loud "All right!" Unable to contain his excitement to their slower pace, Neal ran up the steps, yelling back over his shoulder, "Thanks, Cord.''

Michele murmured, "I guess a station wagon isn't cool to teenage boys. Or isn't *cool* a hip word anymore?''

"Beats me. I just nod my head when they say things I don't understand, and I get by without losing face too often.''

"Maybe I should try that with you next time you say something I don't understand.''

He reached in front of her to open the door for her. "Like what? I've made myself perfectly clear every time we've been together.''

"As clear as the bottom of Bud's coffee cup. Half the time, I don't know where I am or what I'm doing with you.''

Pushing open the door, Cord kissed her briefly, then again a little more intently. Raising his head, he muttered, "You have the same effect on me, although I know what I'm doing.''

"You certainly do," she agreed, remembering some of the things he'd done with her.

Stepping over the threshold, she hesitated in the entryway, unsure where she was supposed to go. Or what she was supposed to do when she got there. She'd been in control of her life for so many years, she was finding it very disconcerting to suddenly be adrift like a canoe without a paddle in a fast-moving stream.

She looked at Cord, who inclined his head toward the door of the room she'd been in before. "I'll give you a tour of the house later. Right now I could use a cup of coffee, and if I know Pilar, she's already got Mrs. Trumble scurrying around in the kitchen."

They heard Pilar before they saw her when they entered the room. "I heard that. Don't you ever get tired of being right, Cord?" she remarked from her position in the chair Michael had occupied when Michele had first met him.

Grinning, Cord replied, "Never." He prompted Michele to sit on the couch and sat down beside her. "I also remember that you prefer tea. Did you take pity on us and order coffee, too?"

"Of course." Pilar shifted her attention to Michele and changed the subject. "Hannah tells me you're a veterinarian. Is that right?"

"Yes."

"How extraordinary. I don't know of any women veterinarians."

Cord interjected, "You've never had a pet, Pilar. Except for that golf pro you used to date—he could have used a distemper shot and a muzzle."

Instead of retaliating to Cord directly, she glanced at Michele. "I was a little concerned about your getting involved with Cord, but now that I think of it, he has the tongue of an adder and the disposition of a pit bull. Perhaps it's a perfect union, after all. You can always threaten to neuter him or something equally disgusting if he gets out of line.''

Cord flinched. ''Michele hasn't had much experience in the Sutherland style of give-and-take, Pilar. She might think you're serious.''

Smiling broadly, she said, ''I am. And I think she understands perfectly.''

Cord glanced at Michele, who was biting her bottom lip to keep from laughing. Then she gave up when she saw the affronted expression on his face. Her laughter bounced off the paneled walls of the study.

For an instant, Cord realized it was the first time he'd ever heard Michele laugh outright. She had a beautiful laugh, very infectious and lilting. He started to smile, then grinned, then began to laugh, too.

Hannah came to the door and peered in. ''What's so funny? I suppose Uncle Cord is telling dirty jokes again, and I have to leave the room.''

Pilar extended her hand toward her daughter. ''Come in, sweetheart. Your sister just passed the test. She's definitely a Sutherland.''

Michele didn't know who or what had done the trick, but she did feel as though she belonged. Even Neal seemed to have accepted her. Adjusting to an instant family was easier than she'd expected.

The feeling was too new to take for granted, which Michele didn't. After all, things could change again once she returned to Nags Head.

That first day, Hannah showed her to a room on the second floor, which was automatically referred to from then on as Michele's room. Cord also had a room for his use for the times he stayed with the children when Michael went on a trip or like now, when he was in the hospital. Cord would be next door to her all night long.

Mrs. Trumble accepted Michele without curiosity or question. As far as she was concerned, Michael's daughter had a right to be there and that was that in her opinion, which she voiced quite clearly. After a brief discussion about Michele's likes and dislikes concerning food, the housekeeper went about her business.

After a brief lunch, Hannah and Neal spent most of the afternoon in their rooms catching up on the sleep they'd lost during the previous night.

The evening meal was fast-food hamburgers followed by eighteen holes of miniature golf.

Each time Michele mentioned that she should get back to Nags Head, Hannah came up with something else she needed her help with, or she hadn't told her or shown her.

The second day went by unbelievably fast, even with Hannah and Neal leaving the house early to attend school. Pilar stopped by in the morning to invite Michele to lunch with her and a few friends and to visit one of her gift shops. Having never been one to have lunch with the girls, Michele surprised herself by thoroughly enjoying dining with Pilar and two professional women who were Pilar's sorority sisters. After their coffee was served, one of the women casually asked how long Michele planned to be in town, and she honestly answered that she wasn't sure.

Michele could give herself the excuse that she wanted to stay because Cord had said her father would want her there, and she could perhaps help Hannah and Neal through Michael's hospital stay. That was partly true, but she mainly liked the feeling of being part of a family unit. And, of course, having the opportunity to see Cord.

When she called the clinic her first evening in Virginia Beach, Bud told her to stay as long as necessary, that he had everything under control except his new wife's checkbook.

When she brought up the subject with Cord of how long she should stay, he left it up to her whether she returned to Nags Head or not, which was no help at all. After all, he'd pointed out, she was the only one who knew the length of time she could be away from the clinic and her mother. Before he left her in front of her bedroom door the first night, he had made it clear he was glad she was there, even if he would have preferred a great deal more privacy than they had in Michael's house. He had kissed her with a devastating hunger that matched her own, breaking away from her while he still could and ruefully wishing her a good night.

The next day, she didn't see Cord again until he sat opposite her at the dinner table, which was a fairly formal proceeding with cloth napkins, crystal and fine china.

Luckily Pilar had warned Michele of the nightly custom in Michael's house, and had taken her to several specialty shops where she found a suitable dress, since she hadn't brought anything but casual clothes with her. Michele was glad of the advance notice from Pilar when she entered the dining room and saw Cord wearing a gray suit and a tie.

The expression of approval in his eyes when he raked his gaze over her nearly made her stumble on the carpet as she crossed the room. The smoldering desire in his eyes was reassuring after spending the better part of the day wondering how long their affair could last if they rarely saw each other. Even being in the same town didn't seem to create any more opportunities for them to be together than if she were still in Nags Head.

She knew Cord was busy with the marina and the other businesses Michael owned separately from their partnership, but she couldn't stop the occasional doubts about their relationship from seeping into her mind from time to time.

Their relationship was like a new delicate plant that had taken root but needed constant attention or else it could die from lack of nourishment. She wanted their relationship to grow and last and be forever. Perhaps Cord didn't want the same things.

When Michele had phoned Faith's cottage after arriving in Virginia Beach, Edith Walcott had reassured her that Faith was being extremely cooperative and there hadn't been another wild run on the bars. At the time of the phone call, Michele's mother was sitting out on the deck with her needlepoint, something Faith hadn't done for a long time. Mrs. Walcott asked about Mr. Sutherland's condition, sending her best wishes along to the family when Michele told her he was expected to make a full recovery.

The second night in her father's home, Michele heard a clock somewhere downstairs strike eleven as she approached Cord's room. She could see a streak of light under the closed door, which she hoped meant he was still awake.

She rapped her knuckle on the door, hoping that he could hear it but that no one else would. She was about to tap again when Cord opened the door.

A raised eyebrow was the only reaction of surprise he gave when he saw her. Crossing his arms over his chest, he leaned a shoulder against the doorframe. His shirt was unbuttoned and had been pulled out of the waistband of his slacks, giving the impression he had been getting ready for bed.

"I was just thinking about you, and here you are," he said casually. "I wonder if that will work whenever I want you."

"Here I am and there you are. Now that we have that settled, do you have something I can read? A book or magazine I can borrow?"

The eyebrow went up again. "Why?"

"I'm having trouble falling asleep. I thought if I read for a while, I might get sleepy. Oh, and would you have an extra shirt I could use?"

His gaze lowered to take in the cotton sweater and slacks she was wearing.

"I could probably part with a shirt, but I can't help being curious what you plan on doing with it."

"I accidentally spilled perfume on my nightgown. It was the only thing I brought with me, so either I borrow a shirt or go without."

He groaned. "You're going to be the death of me, woman."

"Really?" she asked, completely mystified. "Are you that fond of your shirts?"

"I've been driving myself crazy thinking about you sleeping next door, and now I have to think about my shirt covering you instead of me."

A great surge of desire swept over her like a giant wave. She stood in front of him, unaware of the melting expression in her eyes as she looked at him.

"Lord, woman. Don't look at me like that."

Cord made another sound of torment deep in his throat and reached for her. He drew her into his bed-

room and into his arms. The door clicked shut behind
Michele, but she wasn't aware of it. All she could hear
was her heart beating heavily in her ears when he lowered his head to kiss her.

The hunger in him fired her response, and she fed
his desire with her own.

"You feel so good," he murmured against her
throat. "So damn good."

Michele made a whimpering sound of uncontrolla-
ble need when his hands slid under her top and cupped
her breasts. She threaded her fingers into his hair to
bring his mouth to hers, her body shuddering against
his hard length.

She met his hunger with a fierce need of her own,
suddenly ravenous for his touch. As she parted her lips
to invite him to deepen the kiss, she realized this was
what she had subconsciously wanted from him when
she'd knocked on his door. She hadn't been able to
sleep because she wanted to be with Cord.

The sound of a door closing down the hall pene-
trated the passionate fog they'd created around them.

Michele broke away from his mouth and buried her
face in the curve of his throat. "We can't," she
pleaded.

"I know," he said roughly. "We wouldn't be setting a very good example for Hannah and Neal if I
gave in to the tantalizing thought of holding you in my
arms all night long. Let me hold you for a minute
more. I just might make it through the rest of the
night, then."

His warmth seeped into her as she stayed pressed
against him. She would have liked nothing better than
to stay like this for the rest of the night, but it would

be a subtle torture neither would be able to withstand for long.

Out of the blue, he said quietly, "You misunderstood why I walked away from you in the hospital when you told me you cried when I left." He sucked in his breath. "Damn it, don't tense up on me like that. I'm trying to explain why I behaved like I did."

"It's not necessary." Michele made an effort to relax in his arms. "I know how you feel about getting involved with someone. You told me enough times."

"Those were mere rantings of a desperate man as he was going down for the third time. I'm involved with you up to my eyeteeth, lady. As soon as I can get you alone somewhere away from here, I'll show you how much."

"Make it soon," she murmured.

Sighing heavily, Cord released his hold on her and walked over to the closet. He took a shirt off a hanger, stepped over to a bedside table to pick up a book that was on top of a stack of three others and brought them back to her.

Heat blazed in his eyes as he handed over the shirt and book. "If this doesn't put you to sleep, nothing will," he said, glancing briefly at the title.

She met his gaze with a dazed yearning in the depths of her eyes, then looked at the spine of the book in her hand. *"How to Build and Repair the Combustion Engine,"* she read. "This should do it. I might not make it past the first page."

When she raised her eyes, his were waiting, humor and hunger turning his gray eyes into mirrors of his needs.

He allowed himself to trail the back of his finger down the side of her face. "Soon," he promised.

"We'll have some time together just as soon as I can figure out how and when."

She nodded. Clutching his shirt and the book, Michele turned toward the door.

"Michele?"

She looked back at him over her shoulder.

"Sleep well," he drawled, a gleam of self-mockery in his eyes.

"You, too," she murmured hoarsely, then slipped out of his room while she still had the strength to leave.

The next morning, he had left the house before she came downstairs. Hannah and Neal went to school, which left Michele with time on her own. She spent most of the morning outside sitting on a bench overlooking the Lynnhaven River. It gave her a chance to think and the opportunity to attempt to put everything that had happened during the past couple of days into perspective.

Continuing to resent her father for his neglect would hurt him and serve no purpose other than to nurse a bruised pride that should heal. After spending some time with Hannah and Neal, Michele had fallen in love with their spirit, their joy for living, their enthusiasm. She cherished their acceptance of her place in the family. If she was occasionally jealous of the secure adolescence they took for granted, she forgave herself. Her childhood had been vastly different and more difficult, but she didn't begrudge Hannah and Neal the security they and every child should have.

She was looking forward to getting to know Michael Sutherland better, she realized. It was time to put away the past and the mistakes, not to be forgotten but forgiven. Regrets were a waste of valuable time that could be spent in better ways. All she had to do was walk through the door that Michael had opened for her and accept her rightful position as a member of the family.

The one thing holding her back was the uncertainty concerning her relationship with Cord. He was not just Michael's partner but a close friend and honorary uncle to Hannah and Neal. She had to decide if she could accept only his friendship if he ended their affair. If she continued to visit the Sutherlands after their intimate relationship was over, she would undoubtedly come in contact with Cord.

She watched a great blue heron spread his large wings and take flight from the grassy bank of the river, wondering if she should follow the bird's example. If she left now, she wouldn't be raising Michael's hopes to include her in his present family. Hannah and Neal wouldn't be as disappointed as they might have been after she became an actual member of the family and they spent time with her.

She would be the one leaving Cord instead of the one being left.

She stared into the sky as the heron's wings gracefully cut through the air as he returned to the spot he'd left only a few minutes ago. And he wasn't alone. Flying with him was a female heron.

If she believed in omens, this one would be fairly clear. The birds had pointed out what she already knew; life was better shared than solo.

Michele left the bench to walk back to the house, tired of her one-sided silent debate.

Later that afternoon, Michele went with Cord to pick up Hannah and Neal 'x school so they could go with them to the hospital to visit Michael.

Outside Michael's room, Cord noticed that Michele didn't hang back or hesitate this time before walking in with Hannah and Neal, as she might have done a couple of days earlier. Rocky always used to say a race couldn't be won unless you took that first step, he remembered. Michele had covered a lot of ground in a short period of time, with some giant leaps of faith. If things worked out the way he wanted, they would both be winners.

He would like to have taken credit for making her feel more comfortable with her position in the Sutherland family, but he had to give most of the credit to Hannah and Neal. With the ease of the young and innocent, they treated her as though they'd known her for years instead of only days. Both teenagers took it for granted Michele would go in with them to see Michael in the room he'd been moved to after he no longer needed to be in the intensive-care unit. Because they expected her to accompany them and because she wanted to, she did.

The visit was to be kept short by instructions from the doctor, but it was long enough for Michael to be reassured Hannah and Neal were dealing with his illness and for them to see that he was recovering. Cord fended off any questions about business by saying that everything was under control.

Cord looked at Michele and silently corrected his own statement by adding *at least with the businesses.* He wasn't so sure about everything else.

Just before it was time for them to leave, Michael's gaze shifted to Michele when Hannah mentioned that today she had told her biology teacher that her sister was a veterinarian and would come and talk to the class about taking care of animals if the teacher thought it was a good idea.

He asked Hannah, "Did you check this out with Michele first before you volunteered her to talk to your class?"

"Of course I did," she said with indignation. "Didn't I, Michele?"

"Yes, you did. I said I would talk to your class if I had enough advance notice, so I could make arrangements at the clinic to be away."

"Like now?" he asked, his gaze intent on her face. "Cord said you've been here since the day I went into the hospital."

She nodded. "My partner is handling the appointments at the clinic, but he can't keep it up indefinitely. I'll be going back tomorrow. My partner's brother-in-law has a plane and has agreed to fly me back to Kill Devil Hills."

"But you'll come back?"

She knew what he was asking and found it easy to reassure him. "I'll come back."

Michael visibly relaxed and smiled at Neal and Hannah. "I've had good reports about you two from Cord. I'm proud of you." His gaze returned to Michele. "All of you."

Michele felt unreasonably pleased by his praise, as though she'd gotten straight A's on her report card. She found herself smiling at him.

Hannah leaned over the bed to give Michael a kiss on the cheek. "You be good, too, okay? Get well real soon. We want you to come home."

Neal shook his father's hand with the enthusiasm of a seventeen-year-old who hadn't learned yet that shaking hands was not like pumping water from a well.

Before Hannah could tell Michele that it was her turn to kiss their father goodbye, Michele left the room and stood in the hall waiting for the others to come out. She had made some major adjustments during the past two days, but she wasn't yet ready for affectionate exchanges with her father. She still didn't even know what to call him. Soon she was going to have to decide what term to use when referring to him or talking to him.

She had promised him she would come back.

Cord joined her in the hallway while the kids spent a few minutes alone with Michael. Leaning up against the wall, he kept his gaze on Michele's face. "When were you going to tell me you planned on going back to Nags Head tomorrow?"

"Probably tonight at dinner. I haven't thought that far ahead."

"When do you plan to come back?"

"I don't know. A lot depends on how things are when I get back to Nags Head."

"You mean with your mother?"

She nodded, smiling faintly. "Mrs. Walcott said she's been on her best behavior, which could mean the calm before the storm or nothing at all."

"What about us?" he asked quietly.

That was a good question, but since she wasn't sure exactly what territory that word covered, she didn't know how to answer him. She was saved from having to do so by Hannah and Neal leaving their father's hospital room.

Neal was waving a twenty-dollar bill in the air. "Dad gave me money for ice cream on the way home. How about letting me drive your car, Cord?"

Cord groaned.

There was an additional place set at the dining room table that evening, and it remained unaccounted for until Pilar Sutherland swept into the study where they had all congregated before dinner was served.

Hannah was glad, but surprised, to see her mother. "Mom!" she cried, running to hug Pilar. "Why didn't you tell us you were coming over tonight?"

Pilar glanced at Cord, then at her daughter. "I didn't know myself until about an hour ago. Cord called and asked me to come over this evening, so I can hopefully keep you and your brother from burning the house down while he takes Michele out."

Hannah and Neal looked at Michele and Cord with blatant curiosity in their gazes, but thankfully they managed to refrain from quizzing them about what they were going to do. Michele wouldn't have been able to answer them since this was the first she'd heard that Cord had made plans that included her.

During dinner, Pilar learned she would have to help Hannah with her science project, which was due the next day. She visibly paled when Hannah mentioned blowing up a balloon and placing strips of wet papier-mâché over it to make a volcano. Hannah even had a recipe of various ingredients they could find in the kitchen, which, when mixed together, would make the volcano look as if it were erupting.

"How exciting," murmured Pilar, her face an ashen gray.

When Mrs. Trumble began to clear the table, Cord took Michele's hand and drew her out of her chair. "Good luck with the science project, Pilar. Try not to blow the house up while we're gone."

"I'll do my best," she said dryly. "You two have a good time and don't give a thought to me, even though I'll probably ruin a twenty-dollar manicure helping Hannah."

"We won't," he said unabashedly as he walked away with Michele.

Michele had to practically run to keep up with his long strides. "Are we late to catch a train or something?" she asked as she was whisked into the hall.

"Could you speed this process up a little? I want to get out of here before Pilar hears more about Hannah's school project and changes her mind."

Recalling the expression of horror on Pilar's face, Michele chuckled. "Aren't we being sort of mean leaving her with Hannah's ambitious plans?"

"Yes," he stated without a trace of guilt. "But don't feel too sorry for her. Hannah's volcano will end up a designer-original, spewing perfume-scented lava. Get your stuff so we can leave."

"What stuff am I suppose to get?" she asked with amusement.

"How would I know? Whatever women need when they go somewhere. Women stuff."

"I see," she said pensively. "I'll check to see if I have any."

Cord was impatient as he waited for Michele to gather her purse and to get a jacket from the hall closet. He warily glanced in the direction of the dining room, half expecting one of the Sutherlands to come hurtling in their direction wanting something. If he didn't get Michele to himself soon, his nervous system would blow a fuse.

He stopped short from tapping his toe on the floor as she hooked her pager unit on the strap of her shoulder-length purse.

When she paused to look at him, he asked, "Ready?"

She nodded and started toward the front entrance. Cord had opened the front door when Mrs. Trumble bustled out into the hallway, a look of relief on her face when she saw them.

"Oh, thank goodness, you're still here. There's an emergency phone call for Miss Michele."

"Who is it?" asked Michele, although she had a feeling she knew.

"A Mrs. Walcott," supplied the housekeeper. "You can take the call in Mr. Sutherland's study if you wish."

"Thank you, Mrs. Trumble," she murmured absently, her mind already on the phone call.

Michele took a step, then another until she realized Cord wasn't coming with her. She looked back over her shoulder. He was staring at her but making no move to accompany her.

She held out her hand. "Please," she asked quietly.

His eyes searched hers for what seemed like a long time but was actually only seconds before he lifted his hand and clasped his fingers around hers. The smile he gave her was full of promise and something else she didn't recognize.

Michele gripped his hand tightly as she lifted the extension. "Mrs. Walcott? This is Michele."

"I'm so sorry to bother you, dear, but it's your mother."

"What about her?"

"There's no easy way to say this."

"Say what, Mrs. Walcott?" she asked as she clenched Cord's fingers. "Tell me what Faith has done."

After a moment's hesitation, the older woman said, "Your mother fell down the stairs outside the cottage. I'm phoning from the emergency clinic. I think she's broken her ankle."

Chapter Fourteen

The next hour went by in a blur of activity. When Michele told Cord what Mrs. Walcott had said, he took the phone from her and made arrangements for a helicopter to fly them to Kill Devil Hills within the hour. Hannah helped her pack her things and refused to be left behind when Pilar drove Michele and Cord to the airport in Norfolk.

Michele didn't try to talk him out of going with her as she might have done a week ago. Hiding her mother's drinking from Cord wasn't necessary. He knew about it and accepted the situation without being judgmental or repulsed.

To Michele's amazement, Hannah had tears in her eyes when it was time for them to say goodbye. She handed Michele a braided leather bracelet she'd made herself, calling it a sister bracelet instead of a friendship bracelet. Michele slipped it on her wrist and promised she would wear it and think of Hannah.

When Cord drew a finger gently across Michele's cheek after snapping her seat belt in the helicopter, she realized a tear was running down her cheek. "You're such a softy," he said indulgently.

She gave Cord a feeble smile, and he squeezed her hand to let her know he understood.

She ran the tip of her finger over the bracelet Hannah had given her. It was astonishing to her how quickly she had fallen in love with Cord, Hannah, Neal and the idea of being part of a family. Before, she'd had a vague idea of what she'd missed growing up virtually on her own, but during the past couple of days she'd had a taste of what it was like to be in a family group. Once she'd experienced the camaraderie, the sense of belonging, Michele never wanted to return to the lonely life she'd led previously.

The noise from the helicopter engine made it nearly impossible to talk, which was fine with Michele. She had a lot on her mind and didn't feel like making conversation.

After they landed, Michele was relieved to see a taxi waiting for them to take them to the clinic Mrs. Walcott had called from. Cord had thought of everything. Which was fortunate for her since her mind had traveled on ahead to the situation waiting for her in Nags Head. Michele gave the cabdriver the clinic's address and settled back in the taxi beside Cord, who reached out for her hand, which had been clenched on her lap.

"Try to relax," he said soothingly. "Mrs. Walcott told you your mother was out of danger."

"I know," she said, adding, "she's never been injured like this before. Somehow I have to prevent her from letting something worse happen to her."

"Michele," he began quietly. "Your mother has been trying to kill herself for years by drinking. She's an intelligent woman. She has to know what alcohol is doing to her mind and her body. Alcoholism is a disease that can be controlled only by the person who has it. It's up to her."

"So is endangering her life by falling down the stairs." She met his gaze, her eyes serious and haunted. "I will always feel responsible for her," she admitted suddenly. "No matter what changes I make in my life, I feel it's my duty to take care of her. There are times like now when I have to put her first. I'm all she has."

He leaned his head down to hear her. When she finished, he spoke close to her ear, asking, "Why are you telling me this? I already figured it out for myself."

Her breath was warm and intimate against his skin when she said, "I thought I should be fair and give you a chance to back out now before we become even more involved than we are."

He lifted his head in order to look at her with a gaze as searing as a laser. "Is that what you expect me to do, to take off when the ride gets a bit rough?"

She shook her head slowly, her eyes soft and serious. "But I would understand if you did."

Cord looked deeply into her eyes, seeing sincerity and strength. And something else in their green depths that sent his senses soaring.

He brought their clasped hands up to his mouth, touching her cold fingers lightly with his lips. "Rocky told me that when I found myself between a rock and a hard place, I should make myself comfortable. I wasn't going anywhere.'' He smiled faintly. ''I'll be sticking around when things get hard or difficult. Is that what you wanted to know?''

''I didn't ask a question,'' she replied, smiling faintly.

''Yes, you did,'' he returned easily.

She realized he was right. While warning him about her commitment to her mother, she needed to know if that was going to be a problem between them. Even though he'd indirectly stated he would take the good with the bad, he had no idea just how bad the situation with her mother could get.

He would get a taste of what lay ahead tonight, she thought with resignation as the taxi turned onto the road leading to the clinic entrance.

The visit to the clinic didn't take long. Michele's mother had been treated and released.

Walking beside Michele toward the waiting taxi, Cord said, ''Your mother must not have been hurt too badly if they let her go home.''

''This time,'' she uttered. ''The next trip down the stairs might prove fatal if she isn't more careful. And I don't know how to prevent it.''

Cord opened the door of the waiting taxi for her. He couldn't think of a single thing to say to comfort her. He was beginning to understand the frustration she must feel. Faith definitely needed help but there was only so much Michele, Mrs. Walcott or anyone else could do for her.

Michele leaned forward to give the address of her mother's cottage to the driver.

When the taxi stopped, Michele saw that Mrs. Walcott's car was parked in its usual place and every light inside and outside the cottage was on. She quickly exited the taxi and ran up the outside stairs of the building, leaving Cord to pay the fare.

Michele dashed through the kitchen into the living room. A blanket was in a heap on the sofa and Mrs. Walcott's purse had been tossed on a chair. The usually tidy woman had obviously been in a rush. Voices from the direction of her mother's bedroom answered the mystery of where Faith and Mrs. Walcott were. Michele slowed her pace, unsure of what she would encounter in her mother's bedroom.

The door to Faith's bedroom had been left partially opened, and Michele stopped in the doorway when she caught sight of Faith. Her mother was lying on the bed with her left foot propped up on a pillow. The ankle and foot was wrapped in an elastic bandage.

Mrs. Walcott had her back to the door and was placing a folded damp cloth over Faith's eyes, which was why neither woman was aware that Michele had arrived.

"She'll leave me for her father, Edith," Faith was saying, her voice quivering with emotion. "Then I'll be all alone. She's been growing apart from me ever since she went away to college. I've felt it. She's always so busy with her career, and now she has another home to go to, another parent that will take my place in her life."

"Children grow up, Faith. It's only natural for Michele to have her own life. You can't live yours through hers."

After a short pause, Faith asked, "Is that what I've been doing?"

"I think you are so unhappy with your own life, you have chosen to live vicariously through Michele. But that's not fair to her or to yourself." Mrs. Walcott sat beside her on the bed and held Faith's hand between hers. "Do you know how fortunate you are to have a daughter who looks after you, provides you with whatever it is you want or need? My husband and I never had any children. It's one of the biggest disappointments of my life. Now that he's gone, I have no family except for a distant cousin somewhere on the West Coast. But you have a daughter who takes care of you, and you thank her by drinking too much and falling down stairs when you've been drinking."

Faith made a sniffling sound and her voice shook when she murmured, "I heard you talking to her on the phone."

Just then, Mrs. Walcott looked up and saw Michele, who shook her head to indicate she didn't want Mrs. Walcott to acknowledge her presence just yet.

Turning her attention back to Faith, Edith Walcott asked, "And you overheard me mention the name Sutherland, didn't you?"

At that moment, Cord came down the hall and stood behind Michele. Without speaking, he put his hands on her shoulders in silent support. He felt a warm glow flow through him when she leaned back against his chest, acknowledging his presence and letting him know she was glad he was there. The feeling of being needed was incredible, almost as miraculous as knowing he was in love with her.

Faith finally answered Mrs. Walcott's question. "Michael took so much from me when he left. When he told me he wanted a divorce, I wanted to die. He packed his things—every book, every item of clothing, even his favorite coffee mug. After he left, it was as though he'd never been there.''

"Except there was Michele as a living reminder."

"Yes. He'd taken my self-esteem, my dream of happy-ever-after. But I had my daughter. He wasn't going to have her along with everything else he'd taken from me." She bit her lip when it quivered. "Now he's taken her, too."

Mrs. Walcott smiled as she removed the cloth from Faith's eyes. "I don't think she's really left you at all."

Faith's eyes widened in shock when she saw Michele standing in the doorway and a man she didn't know standing close behind her. "Well, the prodigal daughter returns," she said with a hint of her usual sarcasm that oddly fell flat. "To what do I owe this visit?"

Michele placed her hand over one of Cord's and briefly squeezed his fingers before she released them. She stepped into the room and walked over to the bed. Her mother's eyes were clear, her speech distinct. The fall down the stairs and the visit to the clinic had been a sobering experience. "Mrs. Walcott phoned me from the clinic."

"You went to your father's," Faith accused.

Keeping her voice calm, she answered, "I did. Now I'm here."

"Why did you go see him?"

Michele heard the fear in her mother's sulking voice. "I was curious. You wouldn't talk about him and he is my father. I wanted to know what kind of man could ignore the existence of his own child."

An odd glint of interest entered Faith's red-rimmed eyes. "What did you learn about him?"

Watching her mother closely, Michele realized something astounding. Her mother still loved Michael Sutherland. She turned enough so she was able to see Cord, who was leaning against the doorframe. Maybe it took a woman in love to be able to recognize the same emotion in another, she reflected as she brought her gaze back to her mother.

No wonder Faith was so unhappy, she thought. To be in love with a man who didn't love her would be a private hell.

Michele sat down on the side of the bed. "What happened tonight?"

Mrs. Walcott looked at Faith, who didn't volunteer any information, so the explanations were up to her.

"I went to check on your mother on the deck. Along with her needlepoint, an empty pint of vodka lay beside her chair where she'd dropped them. Then I heard her calling my name. She was at the bottom of the stairs holding her ankle. I took her to the Outer Banks Emergency Clinic. That's when I phoned you. After observing her for about an hour, the doctor released her into my care." After a brief pause, she added, "She had my car keys. She was going to drive to Virginia Beach."

Michele shook her head as she brought her gaze back to Faith. "If you wanted to see me, all you had to do was pick up the telephone, you know. You didn't have to go to this extreme."

Tears filled Faith's eyes. She dropped her gaze to where her hands were worrying the hem of the sheet covering her.

When Faith didn't say anything, Michele prompted softly. "What is it, Mother?"

Faith raised damp lashes and looked at Michele for a moment, then away again. "That's the first time you've called me Mother in a long time."

"This is the first time you've been sober in a long time."

A faint flush added color to her pale cheeks. "With you going to your father, I was feeling desperate."

"I went to see Michael because I wanted to see the man you married, the man who was listed as my father on a piece of paper. Part of the reason for wanting to meet him was to see if there was something about him that was the reason you drank. I didn't realize it was because you loved him so much, you tried to drown the pain of losing him."

Her mother shrugged her shoulders as though it didn't matter, but everyone in the room was aware that even after twenty-six years, it mattered very much.

Michele laid her hand over her mother's clenched fingers. "I've recently realized that if I don't speak up about whatever it is that upsets me or don't like or do like, it's no one's fault but my own if no one knows about it."

The tears came cascading down Faith's cheeks. "I know you hate my drinking and, because of it, I have felt there are times you don't like me, either. That's why I was so scared when I found out you went to see Michael. I was afraid you would like him better than me."

"I didn't meet him to make comparisons. I wanted to see what he was like. Can you understand that?" She pried her mother's fingers away from the sheet and enclosed her cold hand between her own. "I wanted to know what kind of man could ignore his child's existence for twenty-six years.''

Her mother bit her bottom lip. "Part of that was my fault. I wouldn't let him see you. It wasn't to punish him, even though that was what Michael thought. I was afraid he would take you away, and I would have no one. I don't like being alone, Michele,'' she admitted. "When you became a teenager, I knew the days were numbered before you went away to college. I was right. When you came home for the holidays, you changed from visit to visit. It was like I didn't know you anymore, like you didn't need me anymore.''

"It's called life. All children grow up eventually.'' She smiled faintly. "Even parents have to grow up sometimes, too.''

Faith managed an ironic smile. "Some parents take longer than others to mature.''

"Some people never make it at all.''

"I want to. I want to quit drinking, Michele. I know I've said it before but that was because that's what you wanted to hear. Now I'm saying it for me. I'll go to that place in Norfolk for counseling and to dry out. I'd like Edith to stay on here if she wants to while I'm gone, then keep me company when I come back.''

"That's fine with me if it's agreeable with Mrs. Walcott.'' Glancing over her shoulder to the man who was leaning against the frame of the door, Michele smiled and said, "Mother, I'd like you to meet someone.''

Faith made a sound of protest. "Michele, not when I'm looking like something dragged through a gin mill.''

"Trust me, Mother. He doesn't judge people by appearances.'' She held her hand out, and Cord walked over to take it in his firm grasp. "Mother, I'd like you to meet Cord Thomas. He's Michael Sutherland's partner in Virginia Beach. Cord, this is my mother, Faith LaBrock."

Cord extended his free hand. "I'm glad to finally meet you." After Faith shyly raised her hand, he took it and held it briefly before lowering it back to the sheet. "The first time I met your daughter, she dove between my legs chasing after a Yorkshire terrier. She makes a heck of an entrance."

"Evidently you've made quite an impact on her, as well." Faith examined him with the intensity associated with mothers down through the ages. "Michele has never brought any man to meet me before."

Cord grinned. "She didn't have a choice tonight."

After staring at him for a full thirty seconds, Faith looked at her daughter. "I believe I now have another reason to dry out." When Michele didn't immediately answer, her mother asked pointedly, "Do I?"

"Do you what?"

Before Faith could answer, Cord did. "Unless I'm reading her wrong, I think your mother wants you to tell her what my intentions are toward you."

"How would I know?" Michele answered spiritedly.

Cord shook his head sadly, then spoke to Michele's mother. "For an intelligent woman, your daughter can be remarkably dense sometimes. Have you ever noticed that?"

For the first time that night, Faith smiled with genuine humor. "Evidently, I'm seeing a prime example this evening."

Reaching into his pocket, he withdrew a small box and held it out to her. "Her father has seen this and approved. Now I want you to look and tell me what you think.''

Faith struggled to sit up a little, and when she could see better, she stared into the slotted box. "It's stunning. Absolutely stunning." Faith looked at Michele. "It's incredibly beautiful, isn't it?"

Michele stared at Cord, who was smiling like a tomcat who had just discovered an abundant supply of catnip. "I haven't seen it."

Cord snapped the box shut when she leaned forward to try to get a glimpse of what was inside. He grinned when she glared at him.

Turning to Faith, he said, "If you're going to be okay, I'd like to take Michele back to her place and propose. That is, if you approve. Financially, I can easily support her and a houseful of kids who all need braces, and keep her supplied with all the gaudy socks she wants. I'll be faithful and take care of her to the best of my ability. I'm fairly easy to get along with, although I'm not a pushover. I don't mind cooking once in a while or helping out with the housework. What do you think?"

For the first time in what seemed like forever, Faith laughed. "I think you're asking the wrong person. My daughter's judgment has always been much better than mine. I suggest you discuss this with her."

He reached down to grab Michele's hand. "If you'll excuse us, I'll take care of that right away."

Without releasing Cord's hand, Michele leaned over and kissed her mother's cheek. "I'll talk to you later. Will you be all right for the night? I could stay and help you through it if you want me to. The rest of the night and the next couple of days are going to be rough while you dry out."

Faith nodded. "Edith and I talked earlier. She's been through this before with her late husband, and she's promised to stay here with me. I'll go to that rehabilitation place you looked into in Norfolk."

"I'm proud of you, Mother. You're doing the right thing."

Faith looked from her daughter to the tall man at her side and smiled slowly. "I think you are, too."

Michele took the time to thank Mrs. Walcott for everything she'd done for Faith and for promising to help her. Then Michele walked toward the door where Cord was waiting for her.

At the bottom of the stairs, Cord turned her toward the ocean instead of taking her to his car so they could go to her cottage.

Puzzled, Michele asked, "Where are we going? This isn't the way to my place."

"I know," he said in a disgruntled tone. "I want you to know I have two dozen candles and flowers on my boat all set for a major seduction scene. That's what I had planned for tonight when I called Pilar to take care of the kids. We'll use them some other time. I'm not going to wait until we get back to Virginia Beach before we settle this."

"Is this where I finally get to see what's in the box in your pocket?"

"It depends," he murmured without clarifying his answer.

They were walking between two houses in order to reach the beach and a dog barked at them for getting too close to his territory.

"Will you slow down?" she complained. "My shoes are filling up with sand."

Exasperated, Cord spun around and swept her off her feet. "Lord, woman, you are going to probably drive me crazy with your questions for whatever time I have left on this earth."

She slipped her arms around his neck. "If I don't ask questions, I don't get answers."

"Well, contain yourself if that's at all possible. I'm the one who's going to be asking the questions tonight."

The wind off the ocean tugged at her hair, sweeping it away from her face and tearing at her clothes. Cord was the only source of warmth available, and she tightened her hold around his neck to stay as close as possible. She had no idea what their destination was going to be, but she was enjoying the journey there.

Cord stopped just short of the shoreline and let her slide down his taut length until she was on her feet again. The full moon cast a wide swathe of moonlight across the ocean, making the water sparkle and shimmer like ghostly diamonds on black velvet.

The only sound to be heard was the splash of water as waves curled over and slid to the sandy shore.

Then Cord cupped her face in his warm hands and spoke softly. "We haven't known each other very long by some people's standards, but we know the important things about each other. The little things, like I prefer white bread and you'd rather have wheat, can all be worked out as we go along. What I don't want to do is to live even another day without knowing you and I can be together for the rest of our lives."

She didn't even notice her shoes getting soaked when a large wave flowed over their feet. "There is a small problem of how we could accomplish that with

me living in North Carolina and you living in Virgin
ia.''

"The place I currently call home is a boat that ca
go wherever I want to take it as long as there's wa
ter." He looked out at the sea briefly. "You have
whole lot of water near you."

"You can't bring the marina and the restaurant
here, too. Michael won't be able to take over the run
ning of his own businesses or the ones you own to
gether for quite a long time. What are you going to d
about them?"

He bent his head down so he could taste her lips
"This is the age of electronics like computers and fa
machines. It's not that far that I couldn't take a trip t
Virginia Beach now and then. All those things can b
worked out later."

Michele fell into his kiss with a hunger that had bee
growing over the past couple of days. The magic dre
her under its spell as he held her tightly against hi
hard body and took her mouth with his usual de
manding need.

He was as desperate as she was and took her mout
again and again until their breathing was ragged, thei
desire red-hot.

Cord broke away from her mouth and rested hi
forehead on hers for a moment while he caught hi
breath and his control. He placed his hands on he
shoulders, both to stay in contact and to put a littl
distance between them.

"So what's your answer?"

Dazed, she tried to focus on his face. "My answe
to what?"

"To my question. What do you think?"

"I don't think you asked me a question."

"Sure I did."

"Well, ask it again because I don't remember what it was. You just short-circuited all my brain cells."

His male smile implied that she hadn't seen anything yet. "Are you going to marry me or not?"

"That sounds like a challenge, not a proposal."

"Just answer the damn question, will you? If you don't want to get married, we'll live together. But I'd rather go the whole way and make it legal so when the kids start popping up, they'll have my name and my protection." His fingers held her securely in front of him. "And I'm going to stick around to help raise our children, Michele. I don't know much about raising kids, but I know what not to do, so that's a start."

The thought of a little boy with his dark hair and snapping gray eyes was too wonderful to pass up. "Can I wear a pair of shocking pink stockings with purple frogs under my wedding dress?"

"As long as I can take them off you."

She smiled. "Is it any wonder I love you?"

"I guess not." He nibbled at her bottom lip. "Lord, you drive me crazy, but I love you."

"I was wondering when you were going to get around to saying that. You know, between all those children you mentioned and all the pets, we're going to need a bigger place than my cottage. We certainly won't all fit in your boat."

"What pets?" he said vaguely. "You mean the two dogs and your cats?" His mind had shifted to more pressing matters that were enticing his hands to touch and caress.

"And others. The children will each have to have at least one pet of their own, and I know of a German shepherd puppy that needs a good home."

He lifted his head and stared at her. "Michele?"

"Yes?"

"You're scaring me."

She chuckled and brought his head down to hers. "The answer is yes. To the ring, to the children and everything else."

Cord dug into his pocket and withdrew the box he'd shown Faith. Opening it, he held it so she could see the ring inside. Moonbeams of light glittered and gleamed off the facets of the emerald set in an oval setting.

"When I saw this, it reminded me of your eyes."

"It's beautiful," she whispered breathlessly.

He made no move to take it out of the box. "You're not disappointed it's not a diamond?"

She shook her head. "I like the thought of you thinking of me when you saw it. Now will you put the ring on my finger and kiss me again before I become hysterical?"

Sounding ridiculously meek, he said, "Yes, dear."

Michele laughed and held her hand out. Cord slid the ring on her third finger of her left hand. Then he put his hands at her waist and lifted her up into the air, swinging her around and around, their combined laughter floating away on the wind.

Epilogue

As Michele moved for the fourth time, she remembered all the times she'd secretly complained about Bud's picture taking. Her partner was a mere amateur compared to her father.

"Michele, that's not going to work. Cord, change places with her," ordered Michael.

Cord grinned at Michele as he changed places with her. Again.

Now Cord was standing behind Neal and Michele was positioned on Hannah's left side. The small triangular flags on top of some of the boats in the marina were snapping smartly in the wind and waves were causing the floating dock to bob up and down. Considering they were standing on it at the time, Michael was having a hard time focusing on the subjects. Undaunted, he continued to pose them.

Michael had been out of the hospital for three weeks and had spent every weekend snapping one picture after the other whenever Cord and Michele came to visit him. Today they had all gone out fishing on Cord's boat to celebrate Michael's news from the heart specialist that he could go back to work half days.

Cord and Michele had made it a double celebration by announcing their wedding date, which was to be in six weeks. Faith would be out of the treatment center and Michael's health would be stronger by then.

As she watched her father directing Neal to stop squirming and to leave his sister's hair alone, Michele thought again about what a good idea it would be for her and Cord to simply elope, considering Michael planned to walk his daughter down the aisle—which meant he would be passing his second ex-wife, who would be sitting on the groom's side of the church and his first ex-wife, who would be sitting on the bride's side. Michele's half brother was going to be the best man and Hannah was going to be a bridesmaid. Michele's friend Barbara had agreed to be maid of honor.

Michele had discovered quickly that there were certain complications to having an instant family.

"Michele, you should be standing next to Cord after all. Hannah, you stand in front of Neal. Stop horsing around, Neal, or we'll never get this picture taken."

Since they were all beginning to believe that's exactly what was going to happen, they resigned themselves to switching positions yet another time. Michele leaned back against Cord and faced the camera.

"Michele, this is supposed to be a happy occasion. Could I have a smile, please?"

"Not if you don't take the damn picture in the next five seconds," she murmured under her breath, plastering a smile on her face as instructed.

A familiar hand stroked over her back and a warm glow changed her cardboard smile to a genuine reflection of her inner happiness.

The adjustments had been relatively easy to make in order for her to meld her life with Cord's. They spent the week in Nags Head and the weekends in Virginia Beach. Twice they had visited Faith, who was gradually coming to terms with her drinking problem. The weekends required some advance planning, and occasionally they'd made the drive to Virginia Beach during the week if there was a school function Hannah or Neal wanted them to attend.

Michele had turned the spare room in her cottage into an office for Cord, who set up a computer, a fax machine and a separate telephone line. Eventually they would have to look for a larger place to live in, but for now, the cottage and the boat were adequate for their needs. Which were mainly to be together.

Cord's fingers found a sensitive spot under her ear and Michele tipped her head back to meet his dark gaze. Cord smiled softly into her eyes and she smiled back.

"Cheez," grumbled Neal, his young face scowling with teenage angst at the carrying-on of the adults standing next to him. "They're at it again, Dad."

Hannah giggled behind her hand and Michael grinned broadly and snapped the shutter. Later, after the photo was developed, he would paste it into the scrapbook and write Family Portrait underneath.

*   *   *   *   *

MONTANA™
Mavericks

Stories that capture living and loving beneath the Big Sky, where legends live on...and mystery lingers.

This April, unlock the secrets of the past in

FATHER FOUND
by Laurie Paige

Moriah Gilmore had left Whitehorn years ago, without a word. But when her father disappeared, Kane Hunter called her home. Joined in the search, Moriah and Kane soon rekindle their old passion, and though the whereabouts of her father remain unknown, Kane comes closer to discovering Moriah's deep secret—and the child he'd never known.

Don't miss a minute of the loving as the passion continues with:

BABY WANTED
by Cathie Linz (May)

MAN WITH A PAST
by Celeste Hamilton (June)

COWBOY COP
by Rachel Lee (July)

Only from  *Silhouette*® where passion lives.

MAV9

Silhouette

S P E C I A L E D I T I O N ™©

WHAT EVER HAPPENED TO...?

Have you been wondering when much-loved characters will finally get their own stories? Well, have we got a lineup for you! Silhouette Special Edition proud to present a **Spin-off Spectacular!** Be sure to catch these exciting titles from some of your favorite authors:

Jake's Mountain (March, SE #945) Jake Harris never met anyone as stubborn—or as alluring—as Dr. Maggie Matthews, in Christine Flynn's latest novel, a spin-off to *When Morning Comes* (SE #922).

Rocky Mountain Rancher (April , SE #951) Maddy Henderson must decide sexy loner Luther Ward really *was* after her ranch, or truly falling for her, Pamela Toth's tie-in to *The Wedding Knot* (SE #905).

Don't miss these wonderful titles, only for our readers—only from Silhouette Special Edition!

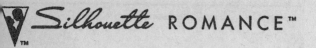

Silhouette ROMANCE™

Arriving in April from Silhouette Romance...

Bundles of Joy

Six bouncing babies. Six unforgettable love stories.

Join Silhouette Romance as we present these heartwarming tales featuring the joy that only a baby can bring!

THE DADDY PROJECT by Suzanne Carey
THE COWBOY, THE BABY AND THE RUNAWAY BRIDE
by Lindsay Longford
LULLABY AND GOODNIGHT by Sandra Steffen
ADAM'S VOW by Karen Rose Smith
BABIES INC. by Pat Montana
HAZARDOUS HUSBAND by Christine Scott

on't miss out on these BUNDLES OF JOY—only from Silhouette Romance.
ecause sometimes, the smallest packages can lead to the biggest surprises!

And be sure to look for additional BUNDLES OF JOY
titles in the months to come.

BOJ1

**Five unforgettable
couples say "I Do"...
with a little help
from their friends**

*Always a
Bridesmaid!*

Always a bridesmaid, never a bride...that's
me, Katie Jones–a woman with more taffeta
bridesmaid dresses than dates! I'm just one of
the continuing characters you'll get to know in
ALWAYS A BRIDESMAID!–Silhouette's new
across-the-lines series about the lives, loves...and
weddings–of five couples here in Clover, South
Carolina. Share in all our celebrations! (With so
many events to attend, I'm sure to get my own
groom!)

In June, **Desire** hosts
THE ENGAGEMENT PARTY by Barbara Boswell

In July, **Romance** holds
THE BRIDAL SHOWER by Elizabeth August

In August, **Intimate Moments** gives
THE BACHELOR PARTY by Paula Detmer Riggs

In September, **Shadows** showcases
THE ABANDONED BRIDE by Jane Toombs

In October, **Special Edition** introduces
FINALLY A BRIDE by Sherryl Woods

Don't miss a single one–wherever
Silhouette books are sold.

Silhouette®

AAB-G